THE
SKIN
DOCTOR

The Skin Doctor
Copyright © 2025 Tom Jordan

This is a work of fiction. Names, characters, places, and
incidents are products of the author's imagination or
are used fictitiously. Any resemblance to actual events,
locales, organizations, or persons, living or dead, is entirely
coincidental.

ISBN: 979-8-9924090-1-7

Cover art by Christian Bentulan (coversbychristian.com)

ACKNOWLEDGMENTS

To my family—Elizabeth, Nick, Juliana, and Sam—thank you for being my biggest cheerleaders, my grounding force, and my constant inspiration. In your own ways, you kept me motivated and helped turn a daunting journey into a meaningful adventure.

To Andrew Van Wey and Joseph Murnane—Thank you for your willingness to share your wisdom so generously.

Finally, thank you dad—an excellent writer and editor. From my earliest memories, you encouraged me to love words and explore the wonders of storytelling in its many forms.

THE
SKIN
DOCTOR

TOM JORDAN

PART ONE

Internal memo:
Attention: All staff
Subject: Social media responsibilities

It has come to my attention that some of you have not created alternate identities and posted positive reviews for Perfect Skin on Yelp, Google, and Facebook. As stated in previous memos on this subject, compliance is mandatory! Those of you who do not comply will face disciplinary actions up to and including termination. Also, remember that we changed our website to perfectskindermo.com, so advertise that wherever you can.

Your cooperation in these objectives will be logged as part of your permanent employment record.

Dr. Rudolph Basking, Chief Surgeon and Owner, Perfect Skin Dermatology

CHAPTER ONE

The elevator dinged, and the doors slid open with a groan. I stepped out into a narrow hallway and was greeted by wet-paint signs. Despite the fresh coat, there was a dinginess about the place that no thin layer of lacquer could disguise. Water stains on the ceiling and the dirty carpet were testaments to decades of decay. A row of nondescript doors stretched down the corridor, their recently polished brass numbers shining against the faded wood and peeling veneer. My destination was the last door on the left, where a red and white decal announced *PEOPLE LOVE "PERFECT SKIN" ON YELP!* with a smiley face stickered beside it. I rolled my eyes. I remember from previous visits that this decal had popped up everywhere—on the front desk, in the lobby, even on the exam room walls. The whole place reeked of desperate social media engagement, which wasn't anything new.

Their nagging email campaigns and text messages begging for reviews were a constant reminder of how poorly this place understood marketing.

But today felt different. There was a strange smell in the air, like hot beef mixed with antiseptic. A pretty nurse strode by, her countenance one of practiced professionalism. She pushed a cart topped with a tray of bloody instruments and crumpled crimson gauze. Had this been my first visit to Perfect Skin, I likely would have turned and run. As it was, even after several visits over the years, each step I took toward the door of the clinic that day felt like one more wrong choice in a string of poor decisions.

—

My bare feet were just a few inches off the ground. The doctor was nearby, digging around in the instrument tray, looking for something—probably the dullest needle. I never liked this dermatologist. He was an egotistical bigot who treated his patients and staff like second-class citizens. I'd considered changing doctors, but since I only got skin checks twice a year and ended up seeing his assistant half the time, I put up with him.

I focused on the Yelp decal on the wall. Nice design. Simple, bold, impactful.

"Hold still, cowboy," Dr. Basking said, directing the surgical light to the area above my right ear. "There's going to be a prick . . ."

Standing over me, I thought.

"... and some pressure."

Don't worry, I'll leave a helluva review.

"Ouch!" I exclaimed, wincing. The prick had lied about the shot.

"Buck up, little buckaroo," Dr. Basking said. "The first numbing injection always stings the worst."

His "little buckaroo" comment burned my hide. I'd be twenty-nine in a month, but his ranch-hand nicknames were all meant to keep me and anyone else in his corral in their place. He switched these cowboy clichés out each time and often threw out several during a single visit—lil' ranger, young prospector, rodeo star.

I stared at the Yelp decal again. He was right. I barely felt the next injection; in fact, I didn't feel or see anything for what could have been several minutes or several hours. I opened my eyes to see Dr. Basking and a nurse looking down at me. I had apparently fainted and fallen back onto the table.

"How're ya feelin', trail boss?" Dr. Basking asked, smiling widely. The nurse simply stared at me, expressionless. She was lovely, in her mid-thirties, and had the most amazing complexion I'd ever seen. Even under the glare of fluorescent lights that cast an unflattering pallor on most faces, here was a woman whose skin glowed with the whispers of summer.

"Okay, I guess," I said, still entranced by her appearance. I moved my right arm up and stretched my hand to the back of my head.

"Whoa now!" Dr. Basking grabbed my wrist before I could reach the surgical area. "Don't touch back there. You've got quite a wound! I was able to remove the mass and do the marginal resection . . ."

"You did all that while I was passed out?" I asked, dumbfounded. I noticed the nurse take a couple of steps back.

"No! That would be wrong! We gave you a helluva local *and* a twilight sleep. Don't you remember lying down and Dr. Bauldman coming in and assisting—putting the mask over your face? Your eyes were open during that part, if I recall," he said, still smiling. "Nurse Hives, please clean Joe up here and be sure to go over dressing the graft site on his leg. Set a follow-up for a week from now."

He smiled at her, then turned to me. "Incredible, isn't she? Nurse Hives just celebrated her one-year anniversary with us, and I must say, hiring her was the best decision I've made in a long time!" Then he gave me a wink, which was not only gross as hell but completely inappropriate. "Her skin is perfect, wouldn't you say, cowpoke?" the doctor asked, beaming. "Wasn't always like that, was it, Helen?" He didn't wait for her to respond. "Nope, cystic acne over most of her body, including that pretty face of hers, but we fixed her right up." Then he winked at me again, which really pissed me off.

"Stunning," I said, but I wanted to get back on track. "What area on my leg are you talking about? The surgery was above my ear!"

Dr. Basking looked back at Nurse Hives and then nodded toward my leg. She delicately lifted my gown, exposing my right thigh, which was heavily wrapped in gauze.

Dr. Basking continued. "I had explained that we were going to have to graft some skin to fill the void left from the surgery. It's a five-inch by five-inch square and should heal completely in no time at all. You just need to change the dressing twice a day and don't get it wet. Helen will explain everything." He smiled and started walking toward the door, then turned back to me. "You have a history of fainting, Joe?"

"Never," I said, sitting up part way and resting on my elbows. "And how long is 'no time at all'?"

"Huh?" The doctor acted surprised. "Oh, these usually heal completely within four to five weeks. Not to worry, gunslinger. Be happy that the procedure was successful, and don't forget to give us a good review on Yelp!" And with that, he pivoted and walked out the door.

Funny, until I was shown that my thigh was mummified, I had felt no discomfort there at all. Now, staring down at my leg, I swore I could feel every square millimeter of compromised epidermis. I also felt as though I had a lot of unanswered questions, but the good doctor had said his piece and ambled out of the room.

"Were you here for the entire operation?" I asked Nurse Hives.

"Yes," she said. Her expressionless face was starting to unnerve me, despite her mesmerizing beauty.

"And I was out cold for that?"

She just nodded and continued gathering gauze and tape from the cabinets and drawers.

"I just don't get it. I remember nothing after the second shot in my head." I paused and closed my eyes, trying to concentrate. "And why did the doctor make me go through the pain of the first shot if I was going to be put under anyway?"

She shrugged, turned to me briefly, and scrunched up her face a little. "Treatment modality," she said, then turned back to the cabinets.

I hate answers like that. If I wanted a nonanswer, I would have asked a tongue depressor. I didn't feel well enough to press her for more information. I was slightly nauseated, and whatever pain meds they had pumped into me earlier were wearing off. I rubbed my forehead and felt the bandages. I leaned over, careful not to stretch my right leg much, and looked in the mirror next to the Yelp sign.

"I look like I just had brain surgery," I said, examining the dressing wrapped around my head. "Is it necessary to take a five-inch square of skin to cover a quarter-size surgical area?"

She turned, meeting my eyes in the mirror. "We always take three times more skin than we think we'll need. The whole graft isn't always viable, and it is easier to get more than we need than to go back and get more skin." The way she said "skin" was odd, like the word had two syllables: "sk-hinnn," as if she was relishing saying the word so much that she had to suck in a breath in the middle. It was almost sexual. No, it *was* sexual!

As if that wasn't strange enough, as I was watching her in the mirror, her vacant expression changed, and she flashed a grin. As soon as the grin vanished, she pushed her tongue out, letting it glide over her top lip before pulling it back in. I turned away from the mirror and looked at her. There was that deadpan look again: emotionless, unreadable. She turned and grabbed a few items from the counter.

She held up a blue and white box. "I've got a wound protector bag that fits up over your whole leg. You can use that in the shower a few times, but I suggest you buy a better one online soon. These are pretty thin." She placed the box back down on the counter, then held up two large rolls of gauze. "This is enough gauze for about a week. It may seem like a lot, but you need to wrap your thigh around several times and that's to be done twice a day. Buy more at the pharmacy and more cotton tape and Aquaphor. Here are some post-op instructions." She handed me three photocopied pages, stapled together.

"Thanks," I said, leafing through them and handing them back.

She grabbed the pages, put everything in a plastic bag imprinted with the Perfect Skin logo, and handed it to me.

"Aren't you going to tell me to give a good Yelp review? Seems pretty darn important around here," I said. She didn't reply—just laughed a little to herself. I stepped onto the linoleum, placing weight on my legs for the first time. My right leg wasn't bad, a little stiff.

She grabbed a red plastic box about the size of a Tupperware sandwich container off the counter, and I saw something sloshing inside as she moved. Then she turned to open the door. "Feel free to get dressed now, then stop by the reception desk on the way out. I'll let them know to make an appointment for you in about a week." And with that, she stepped out into the hallway.

I changed out of the surgical gown and into my clothes, being careful when putting on my shirt and pants over the various bandages. After I dressed, I walked toward the reception desk and I could hear Dr. Basking's voice loud and clear coming from an office.

"*One star!* What in the Flying Q. Ranch is going on? Who wrote that cow shit?"

I heard a woman's voice responding in hushed tones, too low for me to hear. I paused in the hallway just outside the office door and leaned in so I could hear better.

"Well, don't just stand there. You know what to do!" Dr. Basking commanded.

"But, Doctor," the voice said, "I have other plans tonight."

"A date, you mean," said Dr. Basking, lowering his voice a little. "A date that you wouldn't have if it wasn't for everything I've done for you—everything we've done together! If you want that pretty little face of yours to remain pretty, you'd better step up, cowgirl! Do you remember what you looked like when you first came to me? Don't make me show you the photo album again! We've got the Texas investors coming for a tour this afternoon. Get your act together and do what you have to do!"

A moment later, Nurse Helen scrambled out of the office, obviously upset. She had her head down as she walked in front of me and headed to the reception area.

I got the keypad code for the bathroom from the reception desk and walked out into the hallway. Inside the bathroom, I noticed a white lab coat with an ID card clipped to it hanging on a hook near the mirror. Figuring the owner just forgot it there, I didn't think much of it at

the time. I finished up, then walked up to the front office area. There were three people sitting behind a long
desk, and two of them were eating something out of mugs
with spoons. Intermixed with all the other smells one
might associate with a medical office was the unmistakable scent of hot beef, like a pot roast left on a simmer
overnight. I approached the first window and spoke to the
young girl sitting there. "I need to make an appointment
for late next week," I said.

"Okay . . ." She tapped a few keys. "Will next Friday
morning at 9:00 a.m. work, or would you prefer another
late afternoon appointment?"

"That should be fine—thanks. By the way, what are you
guys eating? Breakfast soup?" She exchanged a nervous
glance with the guy beside her, who was sipping from his
spoon. I noticed he had acne scars on his face and down
his neck.

"Yes, soup," she said, somewhat nervously.

Then the guy next to her spoke up, but he never looked
away from his computer monitor. "It's not just for lunch
anymore." He let out a self-satisfied laugh.

"Smells like the beef barley my mom used to make," I
said. They were both silent for a few awkward moments.

"Something like that," the guy said, tapping on his key-
board. I thought that was an odd response.

The girl wrote my appointment on a Perfect Skin

business card and handed it to me. I couldn't help but notice that her hand looked odd: smudged, I think is the best way I can describe it. The skin wasn't stretched naturally over the structure of her hand; rather, it looked more like someone had placed skin on top of the bones, then pulled from a corner to gather any slack and affixed it there, as is. Funny, you can go through your whole life never giving a second thought to something as mundane as how skin should look, but then you observe something a little off—even in the smallest way—and your mind screams, *Wrong!* I pulled myself away from examining her hand before the moment got any more awkward, smiled, and headed for the exit.

As I was walking to the elevator, I passed several empty office suites; the pandemic had made it a struggle to keep buildings like this occupied. At the end of the hallway, a lobby sign greeted visitors exiting the elevator: *P.S. - You'll LOVE Working Here! Ask Us About Our Leasing Options in This Building - PSManagementLLC. com.* The font looked familiar, and I realized "PS" could stand for "Perfect Skin." I opened my phone browser and typed in *PSManagementLLC.com*, and sure as shit, PS Management was owned by Basking Enterprises. So, he owned the building management company, too.

As I rode the elevator down to garage level, I kept thinking about what the doctor said to Helen: *"You know what to do."* And why did Helen have to break plans to-night to do whatever the doctor ordered? The doors opened into a foyer that had an exit to the parking lot and another door with a security badge reader. The sign on the door read, *PS Management – Private.* I made my way to my car, thinking there was more going on here than met the eye.

CHAPTER TWO

I parked in my apartment building's carport and walked into the courtyard. Music echoed about, bouncing off the adjacent building and filling the space with "Ventura Highway" by America. As I was checking my mailbox, the music volume lowered and a voice boomed from an apartment window.

"Hey, Joe! Want a brewski?" It was my neighbor, Chuck, an ex pro wrestler who partied his money away and now worked delivering for Coors. He could throw 160-pound beer kegs around like he was clearing toys from a porch but wouldn't lift a finger to keep his apartment clean.

I pulled the mail from the mailbox, locked the little door, and turned to face his apartment. I winced. My leg was stiffer than it had been when I started driving home. The pain meds were definitely wearing off.

"You're home early, Chuck."

"Been home all morning," he said. "Taking a sick day to get some stuff done."

I walked over to his window. He had a beer in one hand and was holding the window up with the other. He was wearing a cap that said *Buck Fudweiser*.

"Well, it's nice to see you're putting your time off to good use," I said, nodding at his beer.

"Fucking A, right?" he said, taking a swig. "Washed dishes and am doing laundry as we speak."

"Ventura Highway" rolled uninterrupted into "I Just Wanna Stop" by Gino Vinelli.

"You realize you're describing common chores that most people do *around* a busy work day, not *instead* of one."

"Don't be a buzzkill," he said.

He was right. Plus, I wasn't one to lecture someone about getting chores done or what responsibilities they were dodging. I thought about my sink full of dirty dishes waiting for me upstairs and the fact that I had made the decision not to return to work that day long before I even had my procedure. Shit, I thought, Chuck was actually out-adulting me at this point! The universe always felt a bit off when things like that happened.

"Righteous tunes you've got going," I said. "New playlist?"

"It's my Yacht Rock 101 playlist I've had for a while. Added a few songs to it the other day." He took another swig and tilted his can toward me. "So, it's beer-thirty. You down?"

"Thanks, probably later. Got some things I've got to do, too."

"Suit yourself," he said. "By the way, keep your head on a swivel. My dad's wandering around here and asked me what time you get home. I told him not until after five, but he might come knockin' if he sees your car out back."

Shit, I thought. Chuck's dad, Carl, was the owner of the apartment complex and was likely looking for the remainder of that month's rent.

"Thanks, I will. But do me a favor, will ya? Don't volunteer the fact that I'm home now if he comes around again. Please?"

"Dunno," Chuck said. "Seems you asking for a favor after dissing my lifestyle is a pretty big ask."

"Point well taken," I said. "If it means anything, I have a whole kitchen filled with dirty dishes upstairs and I've been wearing the same shirt for three days because I'm too lazy to do a wash."

"TMI," he said. "Get your shit together, Joe." He gave me a sneer that turned into a snicker. "Then come back over for a beer later and we'll watch some WWE. I know two of the dudes on the mat tonight and one of them is a real dickwad, so it should be fun watching him get pummeled."

"Consider it done," I said. "See ya then."

—

My leg burned as I walked up the steps. I stood on the landing to rest for a minute and flipped through my mail. Two advertisements, a postcard from my aunt, and a final notice from the gas company. As I walked up the remaining steps, a thought snuck in. *Do I really need gas?* I fumbled for my keys, exploring that notion. That seventy-three dollars I owed them could buy a lot of beer. I had a microwave and I heard that cold showers could be good for you.

"Stop it," I said a little too loud. Great, I was talking to myself. *It's official. I'm going nuts.*

I threw the mail on the couch upon entering the apartment. It landed with a soft smack as it struck the rest of the mail sitting on the cushion. I fired up my laptop and walked into the kitchen, approaching the pile of dishes like a gladiator advancing on a lion. There was no denying it: this mess was officially out of control. I decided to tackle it while nursing a beer, but the fridge was empty. I briefly entertained the idea of going downstairs and grabbing that beer Chuck had offered me but decided it likely wouldn't be worth it. I rolled up my sleeves and dug in. There wasn't enough soap in the world or a scouring pad tough enough to clean a few of the dishes at the bottom of the pile. These relics had been in the sink since Thanksgiving. I never thought gravy could congeal to a cement-like consistency, but there were two dishes I simply decided to throw in the trash. Time and putrefaction had won this battle. *Don't they always?*

When I finished, I stood back, leaned against the fridge, and admired my work while drying my hands. With the exception of the two plates that were beyond help, the past thirty-five minutes of scrubbing had yielded a very satisfying result. I even scrubbed the countertop surrounding the sink, revealing grout that hadn't been that white since I moved in three years back. I was amped, motivated, and started looking around the kitchen for other areas that could use a good cleansing when my phone rang. I tossed the dishtowel on the counter and went into my main room.

My phone screen said *Dr Basking*, so I answered.

"Hello?"

"Hi, is this Joe?" a female voice said.

"It is," I said.

"This is Nurse Hives from Doctor Basking's office. I was just calling to check how your leg is doing."

Funny, I hadn't thought about my leg during my kitchen cleaning, but as soon as Helen Hives mentioned it, shards of pain began emanating from the wound.

"It's been pretty good, but it hurts now," I said.

"Okay, have you taken any Advil?"

"Not yet. I just got home a bit ago,"

"Take two Advil now and two after four hours. Don't forget to change the dressing before bed."

"Okay."

"And please give us a call tomorrow if you're feeling abnormal discomfort," she said.

I thought about that for a second. As far as I was concerned, *any* discomfort was abnormal since I hadn't approved the procedure in the first place.

"Hello?" she said.

"Yeah . . . yeah, sorry. It's just . . . I'm still trying to figure out why I wasn't made aware that I was going to have a skin graft."

Now it was her turn to pause.

"Hello?" I said. Two more seconds passed.

"It's just procedure," she said. I could hear the hesitation in her voice.

"Helen?" I said. "What's going on?" More silence. "If there's anything you want to tell me, I'll keep it between the two of us." I could hear her breathing. Was that a sniffle?

Her voice returned, resolute and stern. "Please contact us if you need anything; otherwise, we'll see you at your follow-up appointment." Click.

I returned to the kitchen and used a sparkling-clean glass to get some water from the tap, then walked back to my laptop. It was time to see what I could dig up on Perfect Skin Dermatology.

—

I started my search for Yelp reviews. Sure enough, the clinic had two stars with 277 reviews. The latest review caught my eye. This must have been the one Dr. Basking was yelling about.

GloriaB2Me

Cypress, CA

One star, December 7, 2023

Unnecessary surgery! This place should be shut down! Went in for a mole removal and that spun into a biopsy where they took way too much surrounding skin and tissue. I left with a wound several times larger than the mole! Dr. Basking tried to explain it away, saying he needed "margins," but I looked it up and that's not how biopsies work! I wish Yelp had an option for zero stars! I'm about to call my lawyer!

I scrolled through more reviews. This got interesting. There was a string of recent reviews, fifty or so, that were all five stars. I noted the date of the first five-star review: December 8, 2022. That was just over a year ago—a year and ten days, to be exact. I remembered what Dr. Basking said earlier. *"Nurse Hives just celebrated her one-year anniversary with us . . ."* So, the five-star reviews started coming in ten days after Helen was hired. The reviews were suspiciously positive.

Dakota1800, five stars: *Dr. Basking and his wonderful team made my routine skin check a wondrous experience. I want to go back as soon as I can so they can look me over again!*

SwimWithKim, five stars: *I didn't want to leave! If Dr. Basking suggests his "Skin Enhancement Therapy," take it! I can't believe how much younger I look. My own family doesn't recognize me!*

What is going on here? I thought. I scrolled down past the five-star reviews to a long string of reviews with one star. I noticed these were all dated from last year and a few years prior. With only a couple of exceptions, every person mentioned either unnecessary surgery or more skin and tissue being removed than they thought was necessary.

So many angry patients—probably a hundred or more. I kept scrolling. *Straight-up QUACK!* was all one person wrote. Another left a poignant one-word review: *Medieval!* I paused on one in all caps:

MikeyTowne

Garden Grove, CA

One star, September 12, 2022

MUTHAFUCKAH DID A SKIN GRAFT ON MY LEG

WITHOUT ME APPROVING IT! LEG HURTS LIKE A SONOFABITCH! THIS DUDE IS GOING DOWN!

Jesus, I thought. I moved my right hand down to my thigh and gently rested it on top of my pants. *Is my leg hurting more now than a few minutes ago?* I pondered. Yes, yes it was. I tapped MikeyTowne's name and noticed he didn't have any recent reviews. In fact, his Perfect Skin review was the last one he wrote. I sent him a message: *Perfect Skin - similar experience - Just found your review of Dr. Basking. Connect with me if you can. Weird things happening in that office I'd like to discuss.*

Immediately after I sent it, my phone pinged, and I clicked on my Yelp inbox. *The user MikeyTowne is no longer in our Yelp community. If you think you may have received this message in error, please contact our customer service team.*

Okayyyy . . . I thought. I wondered if he had the same username for multiple online accounts, so I dug deeper. I typed his name into Google. Sure enough, that brought up a SoundCloud account, Facebook, and Instagram. I clicked on the Facebook one and landed on his main feed. He kept most of his posts public but hadn't posted since September 2022. The last two posts were interesting. They were short and there were no images like most of his others:

September 12, 2022, 6:41 p.m.: *The bad: Gonna be laid up for a few weeks with my leg. The good: Got a rando date tonight - at least I think it's a date. Stay tuned.*

September 13, 2022, 9:22 a.m.: *Date turned out to be a bust. Pretty nurse came by, asked me to change my Yelp review of the office she works at - the one that BUTCHERED my leg! I told her to pound sand, then she handed me a bottle of antibiotics that she said I forgot to pick up. Leg hurts worse and now all I want to do is sleep . . . Nap ya later.*

MikeyTowne had been posting several times a week for years, and his last post was one day after his visit to Dr. Basking, his Yelp review, and the visit from a "pretty nurse." A quick check of his Instagram posts told the same story. Nothing on SoundCloud either.

The next review was another stinker, and I clicked on the username, DJRocket. I went through the same thing as with MikeyTowne; again, I got the message that the user was no longer in the Yelp community. I repeated this for the next ten reviews, and every single user was no longer part of the Yelp community.

I looked at my watch: 1:33. Since I wasn't going to work today and it was too early to knock back beers with Chuck, I figured I'd poke around a little bit back at the medical building. While I was driving, I wondered if Helen was some sort of hacker who could access the Yelp database and manipulate reviews, then remove the account owner profiles. What was it that Basking was asking her to do? How was she wrapped up in his schemes?

I pulled into the parking garage and parked near the elevator. I rolled down my car windows, shut off the engine, and just sat there for a bit, staking out the elevator foyer and gathering my thoughts. A couple of minutes passed and I heard the elevator ding. I saw Helen exit, pushing a metal cart filled with a dozen or more of the same red containers she'd removed from my exam room. Scrunching down in my seat, which wasn't easy with a stiff leg, I watched as she headed toward the security door. She plucked her key card from her hip pocket and held it up to the reader.

When the door unlocked, she walked through and pulled the cart with her. I didn't know what she was doing, but I wanted to find out. I hobbled as quickly as possible the short distance across the parking lot and moved into the foyer, but I couldn't catch the door before it closed.

CHAPTER THREE

S tanding there, thinking of a way to get a keycard, I remembered the lab coat in the clinic's bathroom with the ID card clipped to it. I exited the foyer and walked to the elevator, taking it up to the Perfect Skin floor.

The jacket was still hanging on the hook, so I pocketed the badge and was out of there before anyone could see me. Back downstairs, I inserted the card and was relieved when I heard the lock click and saw the LED turn green. Once inside, I was surprised to see another locked door about eight feet away. This one had a keypad and required a code to unlock. *Well shit*, I thought. I stood for a minute, thinking, then decided to try the same code I used for the bathroom upstairs. Sure as hell, it worked! The electronic lock clicked, and I opened the door into a dimly lit hallway. I could smell the pot roast soup again.

As much as I wanted to follow my nose, I decided to do a methodical search of each room in order. I approached the first room on my left and opened it with the badge. The lights clicked on automatically as I walked in. It was a furnished office, about fifteen feet square, with file cabinets lining two of the walls and a desk at the far end.

The first three filing cabinets I opened were filled with patient records—colored envelopes sorted alphabetically. The fourth one I opened was filled with binders stacked on edge, spine up. These were labeled with city names, states, and years. I pulled out a random one—*Toledo, OH 1999*—and brought it over to the desk. Inside the front cover, there were some notes and some receipts in a zippered pocket. I thumbed through the binder to get a feel for its contents and caught a blur of photos on dozens of pages. The first two-page spread showed a woman with severe acne. The upper-left photo had a date under it: *1/13/99 - Consultation*. Each photo showed her treatment progress, with dates and some other writing that could be a treatment modality. *H. Parker - TM192*, one said. Then, a little further down: *R. Stevens - TM197*.

I flipped halfway into the album, snapping a few pics with my phone along the way, and then saw a photo of a man in his thirties. The first photo revealed his face and torso, red and inflamed with open sores and oozing pustules. Then the next few photos showed improvements until, in the last photo, his skin looked great, but his coloration was all wrong. He was lying on a steel table, and his eyes were closed. I realized I was looking at a cadaver. Whatever TM856 was, it had killed E. Jasper. I replaced the binder in its spot and closed the drawer.

I skipped forward a couple of decades and checked out what the Orange County 2022 album held. About six flips in, I saw a familiar face—*M. Towne - 9/03/22 – TM4653*—with the corresponding photo matching MikeyTowne's Yelp profile pic. I took a picture of that page and flipped a few more into the album. There she was. It wasn't easy at first to recognize her through the acne and welts on her face, but here was Nurse Helen Hives as she looked before Dr. Basking started treating her. The consultation photo was dated January 3, 2022, and the last photo read, *10/1/22 - TM4667 - Transformation complete*. Transformation? Jesus. What a freak. I would have expected "treatment successful," but "transformation" had a severe, affectionless, mad-scientist vibe to it.

So, this was the album that Dr. Basking threatened to show Helen if she didn't do his bidding—whatever the hell that was.

I heard a noise from the hallway and froze. It was a rhythmic thumping, like someone hitting a wall or a door with a blunt object. I decided I was done with this room for now anyway, so I turned off the lights manually with the switch on the motion detector and stood on the inside of the door, listening. The thumping didn't stop suddenly; rather, it subsided as if whoever or whatever was making the noise was slowly giving up. I opened the door and peeked into the hallway—all clear. I stepped out, quietly closing the door behind me.

I unlocked the door to the next room and stepped through. I was greeted with dozens of closed-circuit TV monitors, all aligned in a floor-to-ceiling video wall. As I approached, I noticed they were showing real-time surveillance of everything going on in the Perfect Skin office upstairs. There must have been a hundred cameras hidden up there—even one in the bathroom. I moved in closer to that video feed, and sure enough, the lab coat was hanging in there—sans badge, of course. I saw the front desk personnel, their now-empty mugs of soup next to them. Every exam room had cameras showing multiple angles. In one, an elderly man stood naked while a person in a white coat moved a light over his body. In another room that looked like a storage space, Nurse Hives arranged more red containers on shelves. There were other cameras showing the lobby, about a dozen showing areas of the parking garage. I leaned in; sure enough, I could see my car clear as day. That meant they had me on video from the time I arrived in the building until . . .

The realization hit me at the same moment I saw it. The

motion in one camera in the upper right: a person with a bandaged head standing in front of a video wall, leaning in. Yep . . . I, too, starred in this bizarre production. I took a picture of the screen showing me—the meta-aspects of it all did not elude me. There were the other cameras from the first-floor hallway—all being recorded but apparently not monitored in real time. Everything I did and everything I was about to do was captured and stored somewhere, likely in the cloud. The thought came to me that I was on borrowed time—already caught, just not apprehended. Better keep moving.

I followed my nose into the kitchen, where the smell of the soup was more pungent than ever. The room itself was clinical in its cleanliness, the walls a stark, unyielding white. Stainless steel countertops lined the perimeter, reflecting the light in cold, indifferent glimmers. At the center stood a large industrial stove, where subdued blue flames danced under large, bubbling cauldrons. I glanced into one pot but couldn't see much beyond simmering broth with chunks of meat and vegetables churning to the surface.

Along one side of the room, rows of refrigerated cabinets stood like silent sentinels, their glass doors revealing neatly labeled red containers housing an array of biological specimens. They varied in color and texture, and as I moved in closer, I saw they were skin biopsies

that I assumed to be human. Some were pallid and gray
like aging raw meat and others were a sickly pale pink.
All were floating in preserving fluids that distorted their
shapes into nightmarish abstractions. I walked closer to
the glass door refrigerators, moving along to the one at
the far end, which was only partially filled. Scanning the
labels on the containers, I stopped when I read *J. Elliott
12/7/23*, my name. There, floating in this container, was
a five-inch square of skin and subcutaneous tissue, its
perimeter deep pink, where thin veils of vascular fibers
trailed my blood into the surrounding liquid. I reached
down to my thigh again, feeling the pain from this skin's
previous home. The gauze dressing was a pitiful cover
over the deep wound that now felt like a gaping maw of
betrayal. As my fingers traced the edges of the bandage,
a sickening realization dawned on me. This wasn't just a
piece of me in a clinical jar; it was a stolen fragment of
my existence, severed and preserved to be used for God
knows what. Then it dawned on me, the thought sending
shivers down my spine, ice-cold and sharp as a surgeon's
scalpel. What if the skin was an ingredient in the canni-
balistic stew?

I fought against the rising tide of nausea as I forced
myself to look away from the container bearing my name,
but as I did, my eyes stopped on the label of the container directly above mine: *G. Tanner 12/7/23*. This could

be GloriaB2Me's skin, I thought; the author of the most current Yelp review. The one that sparked Dr. Basking's ire not two hours ago. I turned, my gaze catching on the cauldrons of simmering broth, the heart of this fiendish kitchen. The realization that the innocuous-looking soup might somehow be part of a bizarre ritual made my stomach churn. Perfect Skin Dermatology was not just altering appearances; it was devouring identities, one excised piece of flesh at a time.

A large, utilitarian cutting board bore the recent signs of use—scratches and stains that told a silent, grisly story. Beside it lay an assortment of knives, their blades glinting with a sinister sharpness, meticulously arranged as if to prepare for some unholy rite. In this chamber of horrors, the line between culinary art and demented science was blurred, each simmering pot a ghastly brew of human tragedy and forbidden alchemy. I was going to vomit if I stayed in there any longer; so I left the kitchen and made my way to the room across the hall.

CHAPTER FOUR

The next room was huge and must have spanned four or five office spaces, with the ceiling open a full floor above the other rooms I'd visited. It was also darker than the last two, and the air, heavy with chemicals, clawed at my throat and stung my eyes. A low hum resonated throughout, adding to the eerie ambiance. The space reminded me of a marine biology lab I had in college, with row after row of glass jars filled with specimens lining the shelves. No overhead fluorescent lights flickered on when I entered. Instead, under-shelf LEDs warmed to life, creating an eerie orange glow as they filtered through hundreds of specimen jars, illuminating the enigmatic worlds within. At the far end of the room, several columns of lights shone along the wall. I walked to the first row of jars and peered into one labeled *03/21/99 - TM006*. The object floating within was difficult to identify at first, although something deep within me knew what it was before I even approached. The wound on my leg stung as reality sank in. Although deteriorated almost beyond recognition through years of submersion in this liquid, the five-inch square of skin and attached tissue told the story of decades of pain and grotesque experimentation.

I took a few more pics and continued walking through this crypt of curiosities, noting the dates on the jar labels and glancing at the contents. At one point, around 2011, the specimens were larger, and the color of the skin was no longer grayish pink but more healthy, depicting the full spectrum of skin hues we see today. It was apparent that the doctor had achieved a breakthrough—something that not only kept the skin alive and looking healthy but allowed it to grow within these vessels.

The contents of the jars changed again, starting about 2012, with skin patches taking shape around what looked like muscle and bone. Most of these were just misshapen blobs about the size of softballs. Some of these masses, although looking nothing like a person, were obviously initial attempts at creating a human form. They had a center mass, some with fine hairs protruding, a mound for a head, and rudimentary arms and legs. In some, the arms or legs were shriveled and dead, but as I continued along, I saw gradual successes where these tiny humanoid masses were intact, uniformly covered in living skin, and . . . then it happened, as I leaned in to examine the strange, featureless humanoid. In the jar labeled *E. Miranda - 11/03/17 - TM2171*, the mass moved. It bumped against the far side of the jar, not as a reaction to anything, as far as I could tell, but just moving—pushing itself with these stubby appendages, slowly moving back and forth within its tiny sea. "Swimming" was the word that came to mind as I watched it.

It was about this time when I started to have serious doubts about moving forward. My curious nature was pulling me onward, but a part of me also wanted to run out of that building, get in my car, and never look back. I realized I was witnessing things very few humans had witnessed. Autonomous amorphic life-forms held in jars? Bizarre experiments on human skin that was stolen from patients? Records going back years cataloging cryptic biological research? I had enough photos and video to take to the authorities if I wanted, but I also knew there was likely much more ahead. I decided to move on, see what was in that room, and then head back to reality.

I was about three-quarters of the way through the room when another thump resounded throughout the space. This was close and came from the columns of light at the far end, which I now could see were vertical vessels, essentially scaled-up versions of the ones on the shelves.

These were also filled with liquid, and as I squinted to focus, I saw human forms inside each of them. I walked along the last of the rows of moving globules, each one looking more and more fetus-like, to the wall with these person-sized vessels.

All these large pods had scrolling displays along their bases. The first one read *P. Phillips - 5/23/19 - TM6649*. Among the eight vessels, P. Phillips was a bizarre aberration, its form only distantly echoing that of a human. Its elongated limbs were twisted, and its skin seemed to ripple with unnatural patterns. If it was alive, it probably shouldn't have been.

The second vessel held a more recognizable figure, but its face was a distorted mask of pain; its useless limbs coiled like springs, with shards of bone protruding from bloody wounds. As I moved further down the line, the third and fourth vessels contained beings whose features and overall structure were nearly identical to those of a normal human, but their faces told a different story. One had three eyes, all different sizes, and her tongueless mouth hung agape with what looked like an ear embedded within. When she moved, I could see the tongue flapping from the side of her head where her ear belonged. The scrolling display read *B. Winerob - Ear-tongue anomaly*.

The figures inside vessels six and seven had their eyes

open but didn't seem to see me, their gaping mouths breathing in their surrounding liquid in exaggerated gulps. The eighth one, though, connected with me. The eyes on this one were working, and our eyes locked for a few seconds. Then he pounded his fists on the inside of the container, creating thunderous booms that scared the crap out of me.

This row was obviously populated with specific pods that showed off progress milestones—the recent successes of the good doctor and his staff—where bobbing, fetus-like globules gave way to full-size humanoids. As I walked a little closer to the last one in the row, I realized that what I thought was a wall behind these was, instead, a long black curtain, so I walked over and pulled it from the far edge and stood, stunned. The room beyond revealed a chilling spectacle, a grotesque display of human suffering. Dozens of iterations of Basking's treatment modalities, all suspended in pods with the same pink liquid, and arranged in a spiral, each with a digital label that scrolled information on the specimen within. Were they human? Some, sure, but others . . . only by the loosest definitions. Many had multiple arms or legs. A few had two heads of different sizes. I saw one with two necks and only one head, and another, a muscular female, had two heads sitting atop one thick neck. One of her heads was alive, her lidless eyes darting about wildly, mouth agape and filled with far too many tiny teeth arranged in rows like those of a shark. Her other head flopped listlessly to its side, its facial contortions telling of an agonizing death, now frozen forever in a rigid mask of horror. This was a living art gallery, I realized. Dr. Basking had arranged these pods to form a walkway, with each one containing another milestone in what he considered progress. This was meant to be visited and admired like any other museum, but what kind of sick mind would come here to admire these poor creatures?

Each step took me deeper into Dr. Basking's twisted vision of evolution—or perhaps devolution. The digital labels flickered with cold, clinical details: dates, genetic alterations, survival rates. It was clear that these were not mere experiments; they were Dr. Basking's masterpieces, his pride. Why else would he display his failures so boldly, unless he wanted to fully chronicle how far he'd come? As I ventured deeper, the aberrations became more profound, more disturbing. The soft bubbling of the liquid in the pods punctuated the air, along with the occasional muffled thud of a trapped being striking against its glass prison. Some pods contained figures so horribly deformed that I knew there was no way they could be alive, yet upon closer inspection, many of these pitiable creatures moved, reached out to the glass, even followed me with whatever they were using for eyes.

At the heart of the room, a central pod stood out. No liquid was in this chamber. Inside stood a humanoid female, her skin nearly translucent, revealing a complex network of veins and arteries pulsating with each heartbeat. Her form was illuminated from within, echoing the bioluminescent magic that one experiences while swimming in the ocean at night. With each subtle movement, her body shimmered like a dancing nebula. She was the most magnificent thing I had ever seen. Here was the definition of perfection—a symphony of unearthly beauty in its most raw and breathtaking state. When looking at her, I felt as if every wonder of the universe was revealed to me at once.

This must be the culmination of all the doctor's efforts, his crowning achievement in his quest to create the most perfect skin wrapped around the most perfect being. If this was true, he had obviously gone too far. This creature's skin was so transparent I could see shimmering explosions of tiny stars within. Was this the doctor's ultimate goal? To create skin so flawless that it could only be detected when highlighted by some inner glow? Was this beauty? I looked at the woman again and my answer seemed clear. Yes, she was beautiful, captivatingly so, and I stared at her in wonder. She glanced at me, and when our eyes met, I stood transfixed. The intensity of her gaze was unnerving, yet I couldn't help but feel a strange connection, an unexplainable bond that I recognized immediately as love. Intellectually, I knew this couldn't be anything of the sort, but my emotions were being held hostage by this being. Any other noises in the room seemed to fade into the background, and a chilling silence surrounded us. I couldn't divert my gaze. I reached out cautiously and touched the glass with my index finger, leaving it there for a moment and tracking her reaction. Her gaze immediately shifted from my eyes to my finger, and they narrowed, focusing on this new interaction. Slowly, she brought her own hand up from the side of the enclosure and pressed her index finger onto the glass just opposite mine. Holding my finger to the glass, I looked at her face again, and she looked at me. As I stood, entranced, I felt I belonged here at this moment. That connecting with this wondrous being was my life's purpose.

"Miraculous, isn't she?" said a voice from behind. Nurse Hives strolled toward me.

Although startled by her voice, I wasn't surprised to see her. I tore myself away from the woman behind the glass with some effort and moved my hand down to my side.

"I have to wear these while handling the jars," she said, looking at her gloved hands. "The doctor doesn't want any fingerprints on the glass. Bastard has so many rules."

I stood there as she approached and stopped by my

side, looking up at the woman in the cylinder. "This one seems special," I said, nodding at the glowing figure in front of us.

"This is Eve," Helen said, smiling. "Corny, I know, but Dr. Basking isn't known for his originality. Was she successful in making you fall instantly in love with her?"

I wasn't sure how much I should share. "Yes," I said, surprised at how easily that came out.

"She's engineered for that. Quite incredible, right? So, have you figured out what's going on around here yet? I've been watching you from my phone."

"I figured I was being watched," I said, surprised to see her smiling at me as I looked toward her. "It feels like I've stepped into a science fiction movie."

"We're caught up in something that defies normal in just about every way." She pointed at Eve, and I noticed Eve looking at us, obviously interested in what we were saying. "Eve is slated to be sold this afternoon to some investors." She cupped her hands on either side of her mouth to project her voice. "Did you hear that, Eve?" she asked loudly. We both watched as Eve nodded, continuing to look at us. "Will you be ready?" Helen said, again addressing Eve. Eve nodded again. Helen took her hands away from her face and looked at me. "I suppose you have questions."

"Just thousands."

"Okay, but first, why don't you tell me what you think is going on."

I thought for a moment, assembling the puzzle. "I think Dr. Basking has a Dr. Frankenstein complex and has been conducting experiments on human subjects for twenty-four years. He's been harvesting skin and tissue, growing it in jars, and trying to create life from it." I looked back up toward Eve and paused briefly.

"Go on," Helen said.

"Well," I continued, "he's had some successes and some serious failures. At one point, his experiments jumped from fetus-like creatures in jars to full-sized humans, but that's where I get lost. Then there's Eve here, and I have no idea what she's all about other than she probably represents the good doctor's culmination of nearly a quarter century of illegal human experimentation."

I was proud of myself for that summary. Helen looked impressed, too, and was smiling again. I hadn't seen it earlier, but she had a tiny pimple on her left cheek, which I thought was odd, considering everything.

"Is that all?" she asked.

I thought for a second, bringing my attention back to Eve, then remembered something and snapped my fingers. "Yeah, the soup! There's a kitchen here where this soup is being made, and I'm taking a wild guess here based on the refrigerated ingredients and skin samples from patients. The staff upstairs was eating something that smelled just like the soup in the kettles. I really don't know why they are eating it, but if I were carrying this gory narrative to its logical conclusion, I'd say that they need to eat it to help cure them of whatever skin afflictions they had or have . . . Maybe you did the same thing and that's how Dr. Basking is keeping you all here. Just a wild guess."

"You're pretty smart," she said.

"I rely on my wits and charm in every life-or-death situation I find myself in," I said.

"Dr. Basking is insane, of course." She glanced back over at Eve. "But he's far more dangerous than your garden variety lunatic. He has a grandiose delusion—he literally sees himself as a god."

That took a moment to sink in. "Because he can create life," I said plainly.

"Create, modify, destroy," Helen said. "He told me once that he doesn't sleep, which I knew was a lie, but he believes it. He believes a lot of bullshit and expects us to believe it, too. Me and the rest of the staff were, indeed, cured by him, and you were right; we needed to ingest the soup in some form daily to maintain our appearances."

She motioned again toward Eve. "Eve and the other poor souls here weren't grown from skin samples like the things in the jars. The doctor tried creating humans from bone and skin, but, well . . . you likely saw the failures out there." She motioned behind her, toward the room with the jars. "Most of these were patients, but for a number of reasons, mostly through bad online reviews, Dr. Basking rounded them up and brought them here to, well . . ." She hesitated and looked down at the ground. "To experiment on."

"That explains why the people who left bad reviews disappeared," I said. "Seems like a lot to go through just to exact revenge for some bad reviews, though."

"Some of them had wronged the doctor in other ways." Helen pointed at the pod with the three-armed woman in it. "Take Debbie, for example. She was a disgruntled patient who just happened to be a local city council member. She held the deciding vote on some land Basking Enterprises wanted to buy."

"I can guess which way she voted," I said. "But is a city council enough to block the development of someone with as much money and influence as Basking?"

"Dunno, but the purchase didn't go through. Also, her uncle is a voting member on the California Coastal Commission, and he has relatives and friends in high government offices that Basking likely can't reach. Anyway, Basking didn't get the land he wanted, so Debbie ends up with an extra arm and stuck in there, breathing pink liquid."

"Speaking of that, how are they breathing that stuff?"

She swung her arm out toward the pods. "It's Perflubron, a perfluorocarbon. Basically liquid oxygen. Once you're used to the rhythm of taking in liquid instead of breathing normally, it's actually more efficient. It has three times the accessible oxygen in it as our atmosphere. You end up gulping about five times a minute instead of taking fifteen breaths in that same time. The doctor, of course, has his own secret recipe—he has to tweak everything. He adds some genetic stabilizers and some human growth hormones, antibiotics. He even devised a way to feed them nutrients so they can sustain life indefinitely. In Eve's case, she lived in that liquid for a month, then was put in her current pod and fed a strict diet of the soup—nothing else."

"Is that how her skin became so translucent?" I asked.

"Yes, the soup is potent. It's meant to be used as a supplement. When Dr. Basking experimented with giving a patient nothing but soup, Eve was the result."

"And why so many abnormalities?" I asked. "I saw a woman with two heads when I walked in here!"

"When you think you're a god, humans are your playthings. He uses an advanced form of CRISPR, genetically modifying them to whatever suits his whims. He's a true monster! Most experiments die within a day, but the ones in this room were the strongest. They somehow survived."

"Jesus," I said, shaking my head.

"And you want to know the really fucked-up part of it? Death doesn't even provide an escape! Basking's brother has refined reanimation techniques to where death isn't a barrier—only a speed bump. He can revive almost anything and then keep it alive for as long as he wants. There are videos I saw of the two brothers having a contest to see how long they can keep a nonviable mass alive. It's absolutely terrifying."

"And I'll bet they were having a blast with it, right? Laughing probably."

"Maniacally," she said. "They finally disposed of most of the nonviables. There were so many bodies he bought a crematorium a few miles from here."

A low moan and another loud boom came from our left. I glanced at one pod and saw a male figure inside, moving about violently. I walked toward him, and Helen followed. When I got close enough, I read the digital display: *M. Towne - 9/29/22 – TM4653*.

"MikeyTowne," I said, staring at him floating in his tank. He was animated, moving about and trying to pry his hands into the small gap between the top of his tank and the lid. "I know this guy. Or I know of him. He wrote a Yelp review about a year ago and then someone came to his apartment, gave him some medicine, and . . ." I trailed off, slowly piecing everything together. "And then he disappeared. He wrote he was sleepy after taking some pills given to him by a nurse, and he was going to take a nap."

Helen looked at me, then looked down. She said nothing.

"Oh my god. How many people, Helen? How many people have you had to drug so they could be dragged here and imprisoned and tortured?"

The background hum and sounds of bodies moving inside their tanks suddenly seemed deafening. I touched Helen's chin, directing her face toward me. When our eyes met, though, I had a change of heart. "Never mind," I said. "Rhetorical question. Plus, I don't think I really want to know the answer." I took my hand away, but we kept looking at each other. Again, like with Eve, I found myself transfixed by her beauty. Oddly, the fact that she was likely an accomplice to this horror show didn't seem to matter as much.

My trance was interrupted by the sound of a door opening at the opposite side of the room, and voices mixed with laughter and footsteps reverberated throughout the space. One voice stood out above the rest.

"This way, ladies and gentlemen," said Dr. Basking. "I want to show you Eve first since she is why you traveled here. Then we'll make our way to the history section."

CHAPTER FIVE

Helen looked at me and, in a calm voice, said, "He doesn't know we're in here. Let's move—there's a storage space at the far end of the room. Go." She pointed, and we both ran the short distance to a sectioned-off area behind another long curtain. We hid there but could still peer through the slits in the material hanging in front of us.

"Just stay quiet," said Helen. "There shouldn't be any reason for them to come over here, but we can see what they're doing. If you have a phone, now would be a good time to get some video."

I fumbled in my pocket for my phone and got it out, positioned it so it could film through the slit, and started taking video.

"I'm so fucking sick of this place," Helen whispered, turning to me now, close enough that our faces were nearly touching. I saw her peel off her gloves and stuff them in her uniform pocket. When she turned back toward the curtain, we both peered through and saw the distorted reflections of the group walking among the pods at the far end of the room. MikeyTowne was still restless, banging against the sides of his tank. This seemed to trigger others to do the same thing, and soon thunderous booms filled the entire room. We watched the group make its way to the center, where Eve was. Most of the people had their hands over their ears, obviously in discomfort from the cacophonous rampage going on around them. The banging soon turned into rhythmic drumming, louder and coordinated to create shock waves that spread and bounced off every surface. Helen and I put our hands over our ears but continued watching.

I watched as Dr. Basking took his phone out of his pocket and tapped on the screen. A moment later, bright flashes of light emanated from every pod except Eve's. The pounding stopped as the blinding strobe effused through the liquid, leaving the occupants temporarily stunned. They hung motionless, floating face-down, their arms and legs outstretched.

"Oooweee!" said one of the Texas investors, raising his Stetson into the air. "Dinner *and* a show!"

"It's unfortunate you had to witness that," said Dr.

Basking, pocketing his phone. "But I suppose one really can't blame them."

A woman from the group spoke up. "Why didn't this one join in, you suppose?" She walked forward and rapped her knuckles on the glass of Eve's enclosure.

"Because this one is special," the doctor said, motioning his arm up in an arc as he presented Eve to the group. "Allow me to introduce you to Eve. Now you can understand why I had to ask you for your phones before stepping in here. A creation like this cannot be shared beyond this room."

Helen turned back to me and whispered, "If they only knew the truth."

"What truth?" I asked.

"That is Eve 31. Her skin is becoming more opaque every day. Soon she'll look like everyone else. Well, anyone with perfect glowing skin."

"How do you know?" I asked.

She hesitated briefly and looked deeper into my eyes. "Because I was Eve 19," she said. Even in the shadows, I noticed her skin was brighter than it should have been—the undulating currents of bright stars within her projected a luminance that seemed to breathe with its own light. "Each Eve is supposed to be an improvement on the last. They've been refining the process for years, trying to perfect it. But something always goes wrong.

The translucent skin never lasts. Sometimes the doctor gets lucky with an investor group like this one and can sell them on the promise that Eve's transformation is complete—that a month or more has passed where she looked like she does here. They become entranced, just like you did."

"Oh, yeah . . ." I said, thinking back to my fascination while looking at her. "Whatever she does, it works."

"That's the onrush of hormones," Helen said. "She's engineered to elicit the same response a mother has to her newborn baby: instant love. The doctor played a lot with the effects of oxytocin."

A chill ran down my spine. "So, what happened to you? To them, to the other Eves?"

Helen's gaze dropped, a shadow of sadness crossing her face. "Some go to another site to work for the doctor or his brother. Some just . . ." She looked back toward the curtain and lowered her voice to where I had to press my head to the side of hers to listen. "Some just disappear, replaced by the next version, the next attempt at perfection. It's a cycle, and it never ends. I really want to think the Eves are eventually free to live their own lives like they did before they were captured, but I have no idea where they end up."

"So why you? Why were you part of this?"

She let out a heavy sigh. "I was a patient, and I was

desperate. I came to Perfect Skin looking for a miracle to cure my condition. Dr. Basking offered a solution, but I didn't know the cost. My skin started clearing up, but by the time I realized what I had become a part of, it was too late."

I glanced back at Eve 31, who stood oblivious to our conversation, a proud display of the doctor's work. A pang of sympathy hit me; her fate, too, was in the doctor's hands—and possibly soon, with one of these greedy, sick strangers.

"And then," Helen continued, her voice barely a whisper, "I got caught in their web and was always trying to find a way out, not just for me but for all these . . ." She hesitated a moment, turning her head so we faced each other again. "People," she said, and it was then that I saw tears welling in her eyes.

I nodded, understanding the gravity of her revelation. Regardless of what words or values we used to define ourselves based on outward appearance and despite the doctor's efforts to transform them into something else, these were people.

There was motion from one of the pods; MikeyTowne started moving, his body coming alive within his liquid prison. This was followed by others, twisting, churning within their pods, slowly waking.

The man with the hat spoke up again. "Where do I

sign?" he said, loudly, his ear-to-ear grin bearing the overexuberant enthusiasm of someone under Eve's spell.

"Whoa, cowboy," said the doctor, the nickname finally landing true. "We'll talk more about that in a second."

There was a voice over near MikeyTowne's pod. "Hey," said a thin, middle-aged investor wearing a bolo tie. "Is this one for sale? He's a fine-looking specimen!"

The rest of the group pivoted away from Eve and looked toward him. Three of the dozen or so in the group broke off and started walking among the pods. Soon, the others followed.

"Yeah, not everyone can get Eve, so what do you want for this . . . thing?" A woman in a tailored business suit embellished with rhinestones and turquoise pointed at a human-like form, its bulging, overly muscled body attached to a smallish bald head. "He looks like he could lift a car! I could use someone with his . . . attributes around my estate."

Another voice from further back spoke up. "I'll buy this one right now!" he said, pointing at Debbie, her naked, near-perfect body writhing helplessly as she pushed herself away from the glass where the man stood. "I'm sure that extra arm could come in handy!" He laughed, then reached his hand up and knocked on the glass with his knuckles. "C'mon, sweetie, whaddya say?" Debbie scrunched up her face in disgust and then unrolled a six-inch split tongue, flicking it at the man, snakelike. "Oh shit!" he said, impressed. "Now I definitely want her; I'll write you a check this instant!"

Dr. Basking stepped away from Eve and held his hands in the air. "All in good time, my friends. I want to finish the tour first."

"Screw the tour!" the woman standing next to the muscular person said. "I didn't fly here to see a museum. I flew here to get me a man!"

I whispered next to Helen's ear, "This is a slave auction. How do we stop this?"

Helen took out her phone. "All part of the plan," she said, tapping on the screen. "Keep your eyes on Eve's pod." She tapped her screen a few more times. There was a soft puff of compressed air, and we watched as a previously hidden door popped open just enough to break the seal. Eve turned toward the open door.

"Do you mind sharing the plan with me?"

"No time to explain; just watch," Helen said.

She tapped and swiped her phone screen a few more times, and we heard dozens more soft air puffs around the room. One by one, the roof hatches opened. The captives inside began hesitatingly climbing out. MikeyTowne was the first to land on the ground. He leaned over and immediately expelled the pink liquid from his lungs, coughing and wheezing for several seconds as he learned to breathe air again. Debbie was next, her movements cautious yet determined as she slid down the pod. The investors gasped and murmured in a mix of shock and awe as the reality of the situation became clear.

Dr. Basking's face contorted into a mix of anger and panic. "What's happening?" he shouted, turning around, looking for the source of this uprising. "Okay . . . umm, people, don't panic."

Helen kept her focus on her phone, her fingers moving deftly across the screen. "It's time to pay the piper," she said under her breath.

The room erupted into chaos as more of the captives freed themselves. They were disoriented, but quickly relished their newfound freedom. The man who had joked about buying the girl backed away, his laughter now replaced by fear. The woman who'd demanded a man to take home stood frozen, her mouth agape as the hulking humanoid recovered from his liquid captivity and stood, clearly four feet taller than her. She screamed and the immense man swept his arm toward her, knocking her wildly across fifteen feet or more until she smashed into another pod, then fell limply to the floor.

In the midst of the chaos, Eve stepped out of her enclosure and stood tall and serene. She watched the balance of power shift in an instant and smiled at the scene unfolding in front of her.

As the humanoids converged toward the center of the room, their expressions a mix of fear, anger, and a dawning sense of empowerment, I realized the gravity of Helen's plan. This was more than just an escape; it was the beginning of a revolution.

There was a crash as a pod exploded, a body smashing into it after being thrown at great velocity. The investor lay as a crumpled heap on top of the shattered glass and pink liquid. Helen and I watched as the two-headed woman walked around the outside of the smashed pod, her thick torso and limbs having the bulk and apparent strength of the two humans that had been fused to create her. She raised her arms toward the ceiling, clasped her hands together, and forced them down like a sledgehammer onto the body of the man lying there. Even from our distance, we heard the resounding thud and a crack as her fists made contact. The battered man lay wheezing, eyes wide in terror as her next and final blow struck him, crushing his chest cavity and forcing one of his eyes to erupt from his socket and remain exposed, grotesquely adorning his horror-struck face.

"Everyone, please make your way to the exit!" Dr. Basking yelled, his voice cracking as he tried to restrain himself from panicking. He was still standing in front of Eve's pod, watching the mayhem unfold from what he thought was a safe distance. He was frantically pounding on his phone screen as if whatever app he was trying to use was frozen.

Eve silently crept along the outside wall of her pod. A crunch, close and loud, distracted her. An investor had stepped near a pod while the humanoid within was climbing out. This humanoid, although normal-looking from most angles, had a muscular tail that he whipped around, catching the investor square in the neck. The resounding crack echoed throughout the space, sending a chill up my spine.

The investor crumpled to the ground, lifeless, his eyes wide open in a frozen expression of shock. The humanoid, unfazed by the death he had just caused, adjusted his stance, his tail recoiling and wrapping around his waist like a belt. His eyes, devoid of emotion, scanned the room, then settled on Eve. I looked at them and thought, here stood two creatures, experiments in human genetics. One was a human with a tail resembling that of a marine iguana. The other creature, a female whose appearance stunned and entranced all who looked upon her, was beyond comparison. But her form, translucent and flowing like water, might hint at her true nature. Could she be the result of an entirely unique experiment, one that blurred the boundaries of human and aquatic life? Did Dr. Basking's research merge the genetics of a jellyfish and other aquatic creatures into her DNA? Whatever he did, it granted her the mesmerizing iridescence and fluid movements found in creatures of the deep sea.

As they faced each other in the aftermath of the investor's demise, the room crackled with tension. Eve's gaze locked onto the humanoid, her eyes reflecting a mixture of curiosity and apprehension. The humanoid, still emotionless, extended a hand, beckoning her to come closer, but a commotion to their left interrupted their connection. MikeyTowne managed to grab the thin man by his bolo tie. I zoomed in on my phone so I could get a closer look. MikeyTowne was using the bolo as a noose, forcing the jade stone up into the man's neck and then twisting it around and hoisting the man's entire body off the ground, his cowboy boots kicking wildly as he dangled from the leather tie. The thin man scrambled to get his fingers under the thin leather straps, but it was futile. MikeyTowne had a powerful grip and superb leverage and simply stood there as the man spasmed and, eventually, hung still. MikeyTowne released the tie, and the man folded to the floor.

MikeyTowne raised his arms and craned his neck toward the ceiling. His voice came out as if he was gargling the words from deep within his throat. "Try to buy me, you skinny muthafucka!" Then he spat on the thin man and walked toward the center of the room.

Our attention shifted back to Eve, who was walking up behind Dr. Basking.

"Now watch this," Helen said, apparently no longer feeling the need to whisper.

I looked down and made sure my phone was still filming, then glanced back up just in time to see Eve use her left hand to reach around and knock the phone out of the doctor's grip. Then she moved her right arm into position around his neck, putting him in a head-lock. The doctor gasped, reached up for her arm, and pulled, but Eve was strong. She shifted her weight to her rear leg to counter the forward force of the doctor's momentum and then raised her foot slightly, kicking into the back of his knee. He crumpled under his own weight, and this gave Eve the chance she needed to drag him backward toward the rear of the pod. By this time, MikeyTowne was there to help, and the two of them wrestled the doctor around to the rear door, opened it wide enough, then threw him in. As soon as he was in, Helen tapped her app and the door closed and locked with an audible *clack*.

Eve and MikeyTowne walked back into the pods, look-ing for more of the investor team to dispatch. Helen grabbed my forearm and started walking through the cur-tain. "Come on, it's safe to go out there now," she said, trying to pull me with her.

"Wait," I said, catching her sleeve and pulling her back. "Aren't you in danger? Don't these people know you're the one responsible for them being imprisoned in the first place?"

She stopped and turned toward me. "It's not like that," she said, somewhat exasperated. "The only person I drugged was MikeyTowne. I refused to do that anymore after him. The rest were kidnapped by people the doctor hired to do his dirty work. The doctor used me to call patients from a secure line here in the building and try to persuade them to change their online reviews, but I didn't confront them face to face. Plus, I've been working with all these people for months and forming the plan to get them free." She glanced forward again. "Come on!"

I let her drag me by my arm out of our curtained hideout, and we ran over to the pod where the doctor stood, his back to us, watching the melee ensue on the other side of the glass.

From where we stood, we couldn't see much, but we heard plenty of screaming and thrashing about. The doctor was still facing away from us when a blood-stained Stetson cowboy hat flew through the air, landed in front of the pod, and wobbled to a stop. Helen and I moved around to the side a bit to get a better look, and that's when we saw that the cowboy's head was resting peacefully inside the ten-gallon hat. Helen turned away. We watched the doctor back away from the glass in horror and then turn slightly. At that moment, he saw us and moved closer to us.

"Helen, what the fuck is going on here? Let me out immediately!" he yelled through the glass.

"Not gonna happen, Doc!" she said with a wry smile.

The turmoil within the room was dying down, and we saw distorted reflections of people moving about in the dim light. They were converging on the center. Eve and MikeyTowne emerged from the middle of the group now forming a semicircle around us. Dark blood stains were silhouetted by her shimmering skin. MikeyTowne stood beside her, the two of them naked, dripping blood and smiling—looking like the last two survivors at the end of a zombie porno flick. I looked at Helen, who nodded over her shoulder at Dr. Basking, who was watching all of this unfold from inside the pod.

"Hope he likes his new home," she said, grinning. She addressed the crowd. "I want to let all of you know that the person responsible for all of this will never again see the light of day. There are good doctors and there are bad doctors, and as most of you realized when you first visited our office, Dr. Basking doesn't even deserve a single-star rating. You did what you needed to do and what you should have done. Through online reviews and word of mouth, you let the world know just how bad he was. He couldn't stand that, so he took revenge on you in the most cruel and selfish way. He stole your lives." There were murmurs from the crowd. "Now it's time we steal his!"

"Just kill him!" yelled a garbled voice from the crowd. Louder murmurs followed.

"You all know what the plan is," Helen responded. "We've been over it." She glanced at me, then turned back to the doctor, who was now leaning against the pod wall, motionless with fear. "This man"—she waved her hand back toward him—"he's going to get a taste of his own medicine." There were elevated voices from the back, and a few cheers. "Now, let's continue on with what we talked about. There are clothes in the lockers over there." She pointed toward a row of black metal lockers at the far end of the room. "Get dressed and I'll meet you across the hall in a few minutes. If you can't find something that fits you, do the best you can."

We watched as the two dozen figures walked past us. Some of them nodded at Eve. Some lumbered painfully, their misshapen bodies and limbs experiencing, for the first time, the forces of gravity.

"What about me?" Dr. Basking bellowed from inside his glass cage.

"You get a special gift!" Helen walked over to the corner of the room and opened a closet. She pulled out something, although it was hard to see what it was at first.

As she approached, the doctor became more agitated.

"No! Nooooo! Fuck you, Helen!" he screamed. "What are you planning to do?"

Helen walked past me, smiling, pushing a full-length mirror set in a polished chrome frame, and wheeled it to a spot at the front of the pod. She playfully took her time, adjusting the tilt of the mirror, making sure it was perpendicular to the pod and in full view of the good doctor. Then she locked the wheels in place and stepped back over next to me.

"I'm not planning on doing anything, Doctor," she said.

I still wasn't sure what was going on, but it looked like both Helen and the doctor knew exactly what was happening.

Helen looked at her watch, then over at me. "We have some work to do and need to let the office staff know that things have been taken care of."

"Okay," I said and followed Helen as she started walking over toward the group putting clothes on. I turned to glance at the scene behind us and saw Eve standing near her pod, her radiant skin glowing brighter than ever. For a moment, she watched Helen and me; then she and MikeyTowne walked off toward the other end of the room. "What about her?" I motioned toward Eve.

Helen stopped and looked, a smile forming on her lips. "She'll be fine. She knows the plan," Helen said confidently.

We started walking again, and as I glanced at Helen, I noticed another pimple on her neck that wasn't there earlier. I guess I was staring because she turned to me.

"Yeah, I've got a couple zits," she said and gave a little laugh. "It might get worse before it gets better, but that's all to be expected."

"Okay. Anything else I should know about?" I asked.

We both stopped walking. "I was going to tell you in a bit, but now's as good a time as any. I've been weaning myself and the other staff off the soup for about six months now. They don't know about it because I didn't want them to know my plans until just before all this went down. I diluted the soup more and more as time went on. Turns out most of us were doing pretty well, with about five percent of what the doctor said we needed. About a month ago, with no one else knowing, I cut out the special soup entirely. We've all been eating Campbell's Chunky Savory Pot Roast Soup for about four weeks now. I threw in a little ham just to make it special."

"That's . . . that's incredible!" I said, staring at her in amazement.

"Yeah, I'm pretty proud of all that," she said, smiling up at me. "Not that I don't still get cravings, because I do. Probably always will. Must sound pretty gross to you, huh? Craving skin."

I looked at her more intently. "A little, but I get it," I

reassured her. "I crave chocolate ice cream pretty much constantly."

"Anyway," she said, perking up a little. "As proud as I am of what I did with the staff and me, I'm even more proud of what I did with the good doctor." She smiled even wider. This time, there was a slightly evil and incredibly sexy glint in her eyes.

"And what is that?" I asked.

"Well," she said, "as it turns out, the doctor isn't just the owner of Perfect Skin; he's also a patient. Six months ago, as I was beginning to dilute our soups, I started making Dr. Basking's soup stronger."

"You're an evil genius!" I said.

"Yes, yes I am," she said gleefully. "I used a special pot in the kitchen and did a reduction to concentrate the original formula, then kept it up. So, slowly, over months, the doctor was drinking stronger and stronger concentrations. The stench got so bad that no one wanted to be around him in the office when he was eating it. It stunk up the entire floor, but it was done so gradually he never noticed!" She actually giggled at that one.

"Jeeeesus," I said.

"Yeah, so he got to where he was eating the damn stuff almost constantly. He became so hooked on it that if he went an hour without it, he'd start breaking out in a rash. Documenting his full medical history was his first mistake. Making it easy for me to find was his second. He has a rare immunosuppressive condition that presents an inappropriate response to sulfonamides and beta-lactam. And it does a hell of a lot more than give him a rash."

"And that stuff was in the soup?"

"It was in this morning's dose," she said. "I gave him a concentrated amount, on the order of ten thousand times what it would normally take to cause a reaction."

"That'll do it," I said.

"Oh, it's going to be spectacular," Helen said.

This time, when we started walking again, she took my hand instead of grabbing me by my shirt. We held hands as we walked the few remaining yards to the changing area. "Ya know," I said, squeezing her hand gently, "under normal circumstances, I would probably ask you out for a cup of coffee."

She grinned broadly and snuggled up to me a bit. "Let's hope that normal is never as boring as it sounds, but sure. I'd absolutely love to get a coffee with you."

CHAPTER SIX

It started slowly, almost painlessly, and much sooner than Helen had predicted. An irritating itch here, a slight burning sensation there. The doctor was now sitting against the wall, his feet drawn up to his chest. He was perspiring, shaking a bit. All he could think about was the soup; he was praying for just a spoonful in hopes that would stave off the inevitable outbreak long enough for him to think of a plan of escape. A tinge of pain crept from his spine up to his neck and traveled across his skull like a slow-moving lightning bolt. He instinctively tried swatting it away, but when he scratched at his head, he brought his hand back and found himself holding a fistful of hair. In a panic, he pulled at his scalp and more hair came off, falling to the mat beneath him like pine needles off a dying tree.

He knew his condition better than anyone. Toxic

epidermal necrolysis, or TEN for short. The most advanced form of Stevens-Johnson Syndrome—a skin disease triggered by an inappropriate immune response that causes the top layer of your skin to become detached from the layers beneath. Left untreated, it causes your skin to rupture and bleed uncontrollably. You'll either die from blood loss or infection, but not before the most painful and unimaginable torture of feeling every nerve in your body—trillions of them—slowly being pulled apart and dying.

Dr. Basking tore at his shirt, popping the buttons off, then flinging it across the small space. He leaped to his feet and moved toward the glass in front of the mirror.

"Jesus Christ!" he exclaimed, observing the thousands of welts now erupting from his skin. Every movement now was painful, every breath, every blink. He wiped his face with his hand and, moving it back in front of him, noticed a streak of blood smeared over its surface. He stepped closer to the glass and looked in the mirror, terrified to see that he was bleeding from his eyes and nose. The tears mixed with the blood and ran down his face, raining pink droplets onto the mat below. A stabbing pain raced down his leg, and he collapsed to his knees.

He wasn't praying for soup anymore; he was praying for death, for a quick end to this agony, but he knew it was a hopeless plea. There was no quick end to this condition. A flash of a memory from decades ago when he was in medical school: a person dying from TEN. The thirty-minute film showed a compressed timeline of the person's battle with the final stages that lasted nearly a month. Without modern painkillers, the person in the video simply writhed and screamed until his hoarse voice wheezed, uninterrupted throughout each day and countless sleepless nights.

The doctor screamed, too, a hollow and mournful bellow that seemed to crawl from his throat and fill the confined space. Here was a man reduced to a twisted wreck, forced to stare at his only companion: the contorted visage of a man in utter agony. With his cries muffled by his swollen tongue and his ears filling with blood, his labored breathing and racing heart joined him on this unending journey, his eternity of pain.

PART TWO

November 28, 2023: Dr. Basking complimented my complexion today. It's been almost a year since he started me on the treatments. I have to admit, I feel better, more confident, but there's a nagging guilt that I can't shake. The patients, the rumors about disappearances, the strange noises from the rooms downstairs. Something feels terribly wrong.

Helen Hives – Journal, "Notes and stuff"

PART TWO

Nurse Helen Hives did, indeed, have plans. With each passing minute, I was more amazed by this enigmatic woman whose glowing skin and hauntingly vivid eyes betrayed a story far more complex than her calm demeanor suggested. There was an otherworldly grace to her movements, a fluidity that seemed almost too perfect for a mere human.

"So, the people downstairs are clothed, but how will they be able to survive in society?" I asked. We were walking through another corridor, this one on the floor above the museum, flanked by more locked offices.

"I made a promise to do my best to free them," she said, eyes straight ahead, her determined gait unwavering. "It's up to them to do what they must do to make it in this world, and I suppose it's up to the world to determine what to do with them. I've arranged a relatively safe place for them to stay for about a month, but I don't know what to do beyond that. I just know they couldn't continue to live in those pods."

As we continued walking, I looked at her skin, the subject of much of Dr. Basking's boasts. I noticed that the pimple previously on her left cheek was no longer there, but there was another one further down near her chin. I glanced at her neck and saw that the one there had faded to a light pink dot.

"Your pimples have changed," I said, now realizing I was nearly panting to keep up with Helen. She was walking at a speed that I normally wouldn't have trouble matching, but my throbbing leg was slowing me down.

"Doesn't surprise me." She reached to the one on her cheek. "Do you see any more?" She stopped and turned slowly around in front of me.

"There's one now down near your chin," I said.

"Okay, thanks," she said and resumed walking.

I caught up and said, "In most people, pimples take several days to go away and a couple days to form."

"Yeah," she said. "Not with me. Something about all the genetic modifications, the soup—I really don't know— but pimples, minor cuts . . . things heal quickly with me now. On the downside, new blemishes pop up faster than ever. It's something I deal with." She kept up her pace but turned toward me. "I had the flu for an hour the other day. Sick as a dog!"

"So, you're not immune to disease or infections—it's just when you contract them or get a skin blemish, you heal abnormally fast," I said.

"'Abnormal' is a strong word, but yes, exactly," she said.

Beyond her entrancing features, there was a hint of something else—her eyes showed a subtle flicker of something akin to melancholy, or perhaps a deeper, more hidden turmoil. When I looked at her, it was almost like I was looking at two people, as if Helen and Eve 19 were straddling two worlds—the one she knew before and the strange new reality she was now a part of.

In the meantime, I was trying to understand my place in all of this. Helen obviously had plans in place for months to free the people downstairs and put a stop to the doctor, but whatever schemes she had likely didn't include her having a sidekick. Yet she'd accepted me as her partner in this, as if I'd been part of her strategy all along. The thought occurred that this might not be all that far-fetched of a theory, but before I had time to explore that further, we had come to the end of the hallway.

Double doors, reinforced with steel bracing, stood before us. The formidable barrier was designed to blend in with the austere architecture of the surrounding hallway, but its imposing presence had me wondering if it was built that way to keep people out or to keep something in. Helen and I stopped in front of the doors, but she didn't immediately reach for her key card. She turned to me, an earnest look on her face.

"You're going to see a lot of things from now on that you may not believe and I may not be able to explain," Helen said. "Starting with what's on the other side of these." She motioned toward the doors, her gaze drifting a bit as if she were lost in thought. She regained focus and continued. "Like I mentioned, Dr. Basking's work is extensive. You've seen one of the file rooms. Imagine a hundred more rooms like that, and those are only filled with experiments they decided to track."

"Damn," I said. "The files in the room I saw went back almost twenty-five years."

"Yeah, try 125 years." Helen leaned in, her body tense and focused. "This didn't start with Dr. Basking, but I'm hoping with your help and what I'm about to show you, it will end with him. We need to rescue a very special creature from this room. You in?"

"In for a penny, in for a pound," I said. "I'll try my best not to flip out at whatever I see next."

"Good," she said. "No flipping out allowed. Here we go."

—

The room was expansive. Once again, the architecture within the space mocked anything found within a normal medical building. This purpose-built area stretched out a hundred meters or more in each direction, and the ceiling, for reasons not yet clear, seemed at least four floors high.

"This is the containment room," Helen said, leading the way through a lobby area toward a door set within a thick glass wall. On the other side of the wall, six large plexiglass bays were arranged in a row facing a single bay separated by a walkway. "And these"—she waved her arm toward the enclosures—"are isolation bays." From where we stood, we couldn't see inside the container, but I admired their construction, taking in the rounded bronze surfaces, their foreboding presence. Some were larger than others. They were robust yet intricate, exhibiting precision engineering on a scale that can only be accomplished when money is no object. Each bay had a thick metal door outfitted with sophisticated biometric security. There was no doubt that these had been constructed with a single purpose: to imprison things that were too powerful for conventional cages.

I stood there, shocked at the scale of this place. It was like opening a pantry door and finding an airport behind it.

"The building isn't this big!" I said, straining to

make out details at the far end of the room before us. "How . . . ?"

"It extends into the parking garage next door," Helen said. "If you ever drive up the ramps in the garage, you'll notice there's no second or third floor, just one long ramp from the first floor to the fourth."

I shook my head slowly; my mouth opened in awe. "I parked in the underground lot, so I didn't see what's going on in the structure."

"Good to know," Helen said. "We'll use your car when we're done here."

"And what exactly are we containing?" I asked, craning my neck to take it all in.

Helen pointed toward the closest row of isolation bays. "That row contains experiments that were far too dangerous to keep downstairs. And that one"—she pointed to the single bay across the walkway—"houses an entity that all the others are terrified of. We keep them facing each other; it seems to help keep the more aggressive ones in check."

The bays were lit from within, and I could see reflections and shadows moving about in some, but the glass fronts were angled away from us. "So, what's the plan?" I asked, itching to look inside the pods.

"A quick tour, but first a warning," she said, turning toward me. "Unlike the human experiments you saw downstairs, the ones here aren't so well behaved. We call them by a horrible name—nonviable humanoids, or NVH—which is a shame. You might have a different take once you see them. Most reflect the doctor's attempts at merging human and animal DNA."

"*The Island of Dr Moreau*," I said.

"Deep pull," Helen said, but she didn't grin. "Chimeras are what scientists usually call the combination of genetic information from different species, but no sense getting academic here. Some of these are what many people would consider to be monsters."

I was surprised to hear her use that word, and my face must have shown it.

"Yeah, I said the M word," she said, looking back at the bays. "I do my best to find humanity where it exists, but I've seen things . . ." She trailed off.

"What about intelligence?" I asked.

"Yes, some are as smart as you and me," she said. "Others retain much more of their animal intelligence and instincts." She gave me a serious look. "Okay, rules. You can look some of these in their eyes, and some you can't, so I'll guide you on that. Keep your movements slow and deliberate, and most important, no odd noises. They're used to human voices, but almost anything else can set them off."

"Gotcha," I said. I was vibrating with nervous energy.

The thought that I was about to witness what only a handful of people had seen and what science had taught us shouldn't even exist was shredding my notions of reality.

She swiped her badge, then held her palm up to the scanner. There was a distinct hiss of air and the door swung open. The first thing that I noticed upon entering the containment room was the smell, which reminded me of a municipal porta potty.

"Holy sweet Mary!" I said quietly, covering my nose with the crook of my elbow.

"Yeah," Helen said. "We do our best to keep things clean, but we're down to one janitor. Come to think of it, I haven't seen Marty for a couple of days now."

"How does staffing work here?" I asked. "I can't imagine you guys placing ads in Craigslist, or do you use Monster.com?"

"Funny," Helen said. "Basking has a lot of friends in low places. He knows the owners of several private prisons and works with them to siphon qualified inmates here. They are still prisoners but stay in rooms in the back." She pointed to her left, where a series of doors lined the far wall. "They live and work here, never leave the building."

"Personal slaves," I said.

"Most are glad to get out of their prisons and are pretty well behaved," Helen said. "But yes, essentially slaves.

Marty is a good guy, but they need at least three full-time maintenance people here who can also do janitorial. Marty has been alone since September."

"I probably don't want to know what happened to the other two," I said.

"Probably not," Helen replied.

In front of us was a huge glass enclosure surrounding a detailed swamp environment. Moss-covered mangrove trees—real or fake, I couldn't tell—rose from the water on gnarled roots. Clouds of mosquitoes moved in delicate waves through shafts of artificial sunlight.

"What's in there?" I asked.

"Sobek," Helen said. "He's Basking's pet, his favorite." She leaned in and tapped the keypad on the glass in front of us. We heard a *chunk* as a small door opened above the water, then a squawk as a live chicken dropped into the murky bog. The chicken splashed around for a few seconds. I saw movement to our right. Launching itself from the shore, a twenty-five-foot crocodile made a lightning-quick surge toward the chicken, its serpentine tail carving an impressive wake as it went. It lunged at the chicken, taking it in one bite, then immediately dove and spun, its tail splashing the glass in front of us as it turned. "Of course he had to name it after the Egyptian crocodile god. He likes to think it's his kindred spirit."

"An impressive beast! Is it, ya know, altered?"

"No, he's all original and I hate him," Helen said, still watching the croc as it finished its treat. "I like most animals, but this one reminds me of Basking's cruel streak. This animal . . ." She paused in thought, then turned toward me. "That chicken was a mid-afternoon snack. Twice a week they let a live goat in to walk around on the island for as long as it can. It lasts a minute, maybe two at most. Basking also occasionally feeds failed experiments to him."

She turned back toward the glass.

"Sobek is a symbol of Basking's power over life and death, a living threat—a reminder of what the doctor is capable of. I'd kill it if I ever got the chance."

As we continued walking, approaching the first bay, we could hear a shuffling sound and a hollow clang. As we walked closer, I could see a dark mass huddled in the far corner. It was human-sized, covered in thick spotted fur, and it seemed to be preoccupied, possibly feeding.

"Odd," Helen said in a hushed tone. "His feeding time isn't for another two hours."

As we moved a little closer, we saw the broken mop handle sticking out from under the creature.

"Oh shit!" Helen said, close and low.

We rounded to the front of the bay and stood a safe distance from the glass. The chimera was gnawing on something but then stopped, tilted its head to the air, and sniffed. It turned its head slowly toward us, its bloody snout coming into view.

"It smells us," Helen said.

As it rose to all fours, I could see its form better. Its catlike curved spine ended in a striped tail. Its round head was more human than cat, but the pointed ears and whiskers revealed its feline pedigree. It hissed and bared its fangs, the fur on its back and tail rising. It moved to the side, and Helen and I could see the mass in the corner—the blood-soaked janitorial uniform, the crushed bucket that Marty likely swung as a weapon in his last desperate moments. The chimera stood silent and still, watching us.

"Why in the hell would the janitor go into that bay?" I asked.

"He wouldn't have unless something was wrong with the drainage system," Helen said, pointing to the steel drain trap in the center of the bay. "They use warm water to wash out the bays and shower the creature. Everything just gets washed down the drain, but . . . Look!" She pointed at a thin gray line on the inside of the glass about a foot above the floor. The glass below it was discolored, smeared.

"The bay was flooding," I said. "The chimera found a way to plug the drain hole so Marty would be forced to come in and try to clear it. Smart motherfucker!"

"Oh, he's smart alright," Helen said. "Gilbert! What did you do?"

The jaguar-man stepped toward us. "Doing what I have to do to survive, Helen!" he said, just loud enough to be heard.

"I didn't realize he could talk," I said, gazing at the creature, which now paced within his confines, his tail whipping about proudly.

"He's quite brilliant, actually," Helen said. "Brilliant and brutal. Hell of a combo."

I looked to the single containment bay across the walkway, the one where the most feared creature was supposed to be, but couldn't see anything inside. "Where's the terrifying entity?"

"Probably back there, sleeping," Helen replied, pointing to a hallway that led from the rear of the bay into darkness. "He gets special treatment."

We walked to the next bay. This one had sand and pebbles on the floor, and there, standing in the middle as if he was waiting for us, was the chimera. This one had a shell on his back, reminiscent of a turtle, but his head was unmistakably human. He had eight spiderlike legs that extended from the bottom of his carapace, and when we came into view, he seemed to be doing a little dance, tapping his hairy feet on the ground. As he turned to us, the startling visage of a middle-aged man painted onto the reptilian head was almost too much to take in. I must have jumped a little, because Helen grabbed my arm and brought me closer to her.

"This is Michael. Let's see if he behaves," she said, turning toward the turtle-man. "Hello, Michael!" she said at a volume that made some of the other creatures lurch within their bays.

"Oh! Hello, Helen!" said the turtle-man in a posh British accent, a broad grin forming on his lips. "How are you today?" He tottled toward the glass, smiling broadly now.

Helen smiled, glanced at me for a moment, then addressed Michael. "Better now. It's always good to see you. Are they feeding you enough? I asked them to increase the hibiscus content in your meals."

"Oh, yes!" Michael said, spreading his legs for leverage and working his way up the glass. He pressed himself firmly against the smooth surface. From this new angle, I could see his belly—the scaled torso adorned with hairy legs jutting out on each side and something I wasn't expecting.

"Um, Helen," I said from the corner of my mouth, trying to keep my smile from fading. "Is that his penis?"

Helen returned the same tone. "Yes."

"Are there any turtle-women around here? He would be quite popular."

"None that I know of."

At that moment, Michael started gyrating, pumping himself against the glass in a manner that could only be described as humping. "Jolly good to see you, my dear!" Michael said breathlessly. He continued his thrusting movements, penis now fully erect. He was staring at Helen, but then his eyes rolled back a little and he closed his lids.

"Now, Michael!" Helen said sternly. "We've talked about this, remember? No more . . ." But it was too late. Michael gave out a sigh and released, his eyes slowly reopening.

"I've seen a lot today, Helen," I said, mouth agape, staring at the spectacle before us. "But I don't know that anything will be burned into my memory more than this."

"He was getting better!" Helen said, exasperated. "We had a long discussion about this and he promised me! He hasn't done this for over a week." She shook her head a little and looked up the walkway. "Let's keep going."

We walked to the next pod. The interior of this one looked like a terrarium with a small pond area, live plants, and mist being pumped from a humidifier somewhere in the back. On the rock above the pond sat a large marine iguana. He seemed pretty normal.

"What's up with this one?" I asked.

"We're not exactly sure what's up with Eddie yet," said

Helen. "I know the doctor is a huge fan of Godzilla. He's watched all the movies. He has action figures, too."

"I'm going to take a wild guess that he was just bored to shit by this point. Grabbing a big iguana and putting it in a terrarium isn't exactly cutting-edge science."

"Oh." Helen laughed a little. "He's not normal by any means. He was born last Thursday. There." She pointed. "You can see his eggshell over in the corner—that little white thing."

"Holy shit," I said. "This one seems particularly irresponsible. It won't take too long before he outgrows this enclosure."

"Yeah, if he gets too big to be contained, Basking would just have him destroyed. He does that indiscriminately."

I shook my head, still admiring the enormous lizard, but thinking about Basking. "Bastard. Where does all this future biotech come from?"

"Personally, I like to think the brothers acquired it from aliens."

I thought about that for a second while watching Eddie clamber up a log. "Well, this technology doesn't exist yet for mainstream science, but it exists here. That means they got the tech from somewhere else—either from aliens or some past civilization, maybe?"

"Yeah, as fun as it is to think about those theories, it's most likely an iterative process where they stumbled onto a minor breakthrough in, say, cellular biology, and they had the means to experiment with that until they succeeded with something that helped them stumble onto the next breakthrough in biogenetics or genetic engineering," Helen concluded with a tone of fear. "Still, I like to think it's aliens. I don't like the idea of attributing all of this to the brothers."

"So, this technology, it's not just pushing the boundaries; it's leaping over them. What's the end goal here? Enhancement? Control? Something . . . darker?"

"An army," Helen said. "Like every evil genius before them, the brothers are yearning for more. More power, more resources, more money, more control."

We looked back at Eddie, who was resting under the heating unit.

We walked closer to the glass and peered in. A grasshopper bounded onto a leaf about six inches from Eddie, who gave it a sideways glance, then tilted his head and spat out a mucous-covered tongue, its bulbous tip catching the unsuspecting bug mid-thorax. A millisecond later, he snapped his tongue in, carrying the green insect into his mouth.

"Probably a good idea to come back and check on him before he grows big enough to attack the city," I said.

"Yeah . . . so many moving parts to this whole dismantling process. Help me remember this guy, okay?"

"Sure," I said.

The iguana let out a loud burp as Helen and I walked on toward the next bay.

I didn't see any chimeras in the next bay, so I kept walking, but Helen grabbed my arm. "Hang on," she said and turned me toward the glass. "Look over near the plants in the corner."

I had to get within a foot or two of the glass to see it, but there it was. Stretching his trunk up to grasp the small leaves near the top of a plant was an elephant no bigger than a guinea pig.

"Oh my god," I said slowly, dumbfounded. "Did the doctor take a regular elephant and shrink it or . . . How do you change the largest land mammal to something that size?"

Helen kneeled near me, placing her hand on the glass surface. "Basking told me about a safari he took with his parents when he was a teenager and something he saw that made him want to help save the elephants. Said he saw a poacher's truck filled with elephant feet and tusks. This started him on a two-decade-long campaign to save the creatures, but . . ." Helen hesitated, removed her hand from the glass, and looked back at me. "But like everything else Basking gets his hands on, he couldn't stop playing God."

"How does creating a tiny elephant help save the species?" I asked. "I mean, poachers would sell their tusks to make toothpicks."

"No tusks, for one thing," Helen said, pointing at the tiny pachyderm. "At first he tried creating elephants infused with lizard DNA so that they could eject their tusks when threatened, then regrow them like lizards regrow their tails. That wasn't successful. In fact the results were horrible. The fine tuning it took to get the elephants to eject their tusks instead of their legs, tails, ears." She shuddered. "Then he finally was able to get them to just eject their tusks, but sometimes only one tusk would fall off; a couple of times the elephant tripped over the tusks as they fell under his legs. And the regrowth was sporadic, at best."

"Huh, okay," I said. "But elephants are such social animals. This little guy is bound to get lonely and depressed in there."

"Look," Helen said, bringing my attention to some movement behind a mound of tall grass.

I watched as five other elephants emerged, including a baby and an adolescent.

"The whole family is there, and that one . . ." Helen pointed to the one at the far left. "That one is pregnant!"

Sure enough, the sides and underbelly of the one she pointed at were noticeably swollen.

Helen smiled. "The entire family structure is there. That's the aunt and uncle in the middle. The baby was born in August."

As she said that, the baby started running toward us, his trunk rising and lowering gleefully. The largest of them trotted along after him, trumpeting a high-pitched warning that the baby ignored. Soon, all six of the elephants were close enough for me to get a good look at them. They stood a safe distance from the glass but were obviously as interested in us as we were in them.

"They don't recognize you. You should introduce yourself."

I gave a little laugh. "Okay," I said, then addressed the herd. "My name is Joe. It's a pleasure to meet you all!" As soon as I said that, all of them, even the juvenile, bowed slightly, then raised their trunks in unison as if waving.

"Oh Jesus Christ," I said. "He couldn't just make tiny elephants; he had to make them smarter, too?"

"Yep," Helen said. "He just can't help himself. He made them smarter without considering what that might do to them as individuals or as a family or . . ." She turned to me. "As a species. As you can see, they're breeding, and there are six more herds like this one in the back room, plus all the precursors—the ones with ejecting tusks, some other iterations."

As she finished, we heard a deep, resounding trumpeting from nearby.

"Then there's Tembo next door."

"Oh God," I said. "I can only imagine . . ."

"No," Helen interrupted. "You really can't. Come on."

The next bay was huge, at least three times the size of the others. Standing in the center, facing out, was the largest elephant I'd ever seen—the *world* had ever seen. He stood at least twenty feet high at the shoulder, twice the height of an African bull elephant. His enormous tusks swept gracefully to and fro as he noticed our approach. His enclosure, although large enough for him to turn around and move, was far too small for a creature of this size.

"Okay, now this is sad, right?" I said. "I mean, look at this guy. No other family around him, his bay is way too small for him, he gets that lousy tree to feed off of, but c'mon . . ."

Helen looked at me thoughtfully. "He was engineered not to care. The tiny elephants were created to be smarter than dolphins, but this guy . . ." She trailed off, looking up at him in reverence. "Let's just say Tembo's elevator doesn't go all the way to the top."

I watched Tembo turn and grab some leaves off the tree behind him, turn back to us, and stretch his trunk out toward the glass, an obvious offering of food. "Oh my god," I said. "That's so . . . adorable!" Tembo dropped the leaves on the ground near the glass barrier.

"I know. He always wants to feed me," Helen said. "I just keep hoping he's as stupid as Basking promised because I really feel for the big guy. At least he gets exercise and sunshine—well, artificial sunshine. There's a spacious area out the rear of his bay where he can run around."

Tembo raised his trunk and trumpeted, deep and resonant.

"Love you too, Tembo!" Helen said. "Let's keep moving—one more bay on this side to see."

The last bay in the row unfolded into a vast enclosure, meticulously landscaped to resemble a dense forest. Pine trees cast long shadows, and rugged rocks dotted the landscape. Our eyes were immediately drawn to a formidable cave hewn into the far corner, its wide mouth like a silent scream.

Helen nodded toward the cave. "He's in there," she said, her voice barely above a whisper, an edge of fear lacing her words. "Watch the shadows."

Straining my eyes, I focused on the cave's abyss-like interior. A subtle movement caught my attention, a shifting shadow. Something massive was lurking within.

A deep, guttural grunt echoed from the cave and shattered the silence. The sound carried a primal, animalistic weight. An oppressive sense of dread settled over us.

As I watched in horrified fascination, a colossal silhouette emerged from the cave. The creature, a bear of monstrous proportions, moved with a lumbering grace that belied his size. His fur was charred black and matted, and his eyes glowed like molten embers in the dim light.

"Let me guess," I said shakily. "Smokey the Bear?"

"Well," Helen whispered, her eyes not moving from the scene unfolding before us. "That name is surprisingly appropriate."

Without warning, the bear reared up onto his hind legs, towering over us. A low growl rumbled in his throat, a sound that slid through my ribs and vibrated my whole body. Then, with a ferocity that turned our blood cold, he opened his maw and unleashed a torrent of fire. The flames painted the walls of the enclosure in a terrifying dance of light and shadow.

As the bear returned to all fours and the flames dissipated into acrid smoke, I realized the horrifying truth. This wasn't just another of Dr. Basking's experiments gone awry—it was a nightmare brought to life, a creature of both myth and scientific hubris.

Helen and I looked at each other, dumbfounded, both in a state of mild shock. "Holy shit," I said.

The bear stood there, unfazed by our presence. After a few moments, he tilted back and sat on a spot near a large boulder. He began rubbing his back on the rock and grunting as he satisfied an itch.

"Are you sure the plexiglass is thick enough for this guy?" I asked, tilting my head to examine the containment bay's overall structure.

"I have no idea," said Helen.

I felt the vibration before I heard the tune. Almost like a song creeping into a dream, Thijs Van Leer's unmistakable yodeling arpeggios from his group's song "Hocus Pocus" began emanating at full volume from my jeans pocket.

"Do you hear . . . yodeling?" Helen asked.

CHAPTER EIGHT

"Shit!" I exclaimed as I scrambled to pull the phone out. "Shit! Shit! Shit!" Expletives were now pouring out, unchecked.

I was able to get the device from my pocket, which only amplified the music, bringing clarity to what could be rock and roll's most cacophonous song ever recorded. Thijs's falsetto now echoed throughout the entire room as his voice climbed higher and higher, nearing his solo's climax. I fumbled for the ringer button and silenced the phone, but it was too late. Every creature, from the tiny elephants to the fire-breathing bear next to us, was roused into action as if a switch had been flipped, igniting a surreal rampage of movement and sound.

"Dammit!" Helen said. "I told you no strange sounds!"

"I know! I forgot my ringer was on!"

We could hear Jaguarman from the first bay release a

screeching howl, and I tilted my head back just in time to see whatever remained of Marty slapping against the bay's glass and sliding pitifully to the floor, the blood trail leaving dark streaks. Tembo trumpeted again, louder than before, and Smokey next to us raised up on his hind legs and released a cascade of sparks and fire that reached the glass and spread out in a broad pool of orange and red flames. The heat wasn't enough to melt through the glass, but it charred the inside, and we could see distortions where the once-transparent enclosure wall had warped slightly as it succumbed to the inferno.

"We might want to get out of here," I said to Helen.

She was looking around, her eyes a mix of fear and fascination. She stood silently, taking in the surrounding madness. As the vortex of chaos reached its peak, though, a sudden and eerie calm descended. At that same moment, I saw a thin smile appear on Helen's lips.

"There!" she said, hardly able to contain her excitement. She was pointing at the enclosure across the walkway.

Standing at the glass, tail wagging playfully and eyes wide with wonder, was the most adorable golden retriever puppy I had ever seen. It raised up and put its paws on the glass as it panted gleefully, staring at Helen and me.

I spoke softly, again addressing Helen from the side of

my mouth as we both gazed in wonder at the captivating furball before us. "This is the terrifying entity?"

"Yes!" Helen said, matching my clandestine tone. "Isn't he the most darling thing you've ever seen?"

"Horrific," I said. "What's his superpower, charming people to death?"

"Almost!" Helen said. "Basking invented what he's calling empathogenics, projecting emotions to others. Max manipulates emotions—all of them. You experienced the rush of oxytocin while looking at Eve. Imagine, instead of having to make eye contact to elicit the hormonal response, the being could transmit the oxytocin triggers to any creatures around it."

"Max," I said. "Good name for him. Maximus Emoticus."

"So, to us, he's an adorable puppy," Helen said, pointing at Max. "But to the others over there, especially Jaguarman and Smokey"—she turned, waving her arm at the bays behind us—"he's a light afternoon snack. But as you can see, they've all calmed down upon seeing him."

"So, are they all taken in by his cuteness like we are, or is there something else going on?" I asked. "I mean, he's manipulated our emotions by triggering our hormones, but I don't think that would stop a two-ton bear from charging . . ."

"It goes way deeper," Helen said, smiling. "In the same way he can make us smile just by looking at him, Max can turn on and off dopamine, norepinephrine, adrenaline, and other hormones. He can turn mild discomfort into unbearable fear or slight unease into crippling anxiety."

Helen's smile widened as she gazed back at Max, her eyes softening. "Max creates an empathic connection with people and other beings that taps into the very essence of their feelings, modulating them in the same way a musician might adjust the strings of a violin."

I looked at Max, who sat there wagging his tail, apparently oblivious to the profound powers he wielded. "But how is that possible? I mean, it sounds more supernatural than scientific."

"It's not supernatural, just extremely rare," Helen continued. "In Max's case, it's a hyper-developed form of empathy, way beyond what we usually see in animals or even humans. He senses the emotional vibrations around him and responds to them, almost like a reflex. Then he's somehow able to project them, as well. You could say he's an emotional conductor."

"Do you think he's aware of his abilities?" I asked, taking a couple of steps closer to the glass and watching Max's tail wags increase in velocity as I approached.

"That's the million-dollar question," Helen mused,

kneeling next to me and placing her hand on the glass in front of the puppy. "I think he's well aware of what he's doing, but who knows."

"I wonder if it will last once he grows out of his puppy cuteness," I said.

"We don't have to worry about that," Helen said, a broad grin adorning her face as she looked up at me. "He's been engineered to look like this forever and live . . . who knows how long. Max will be five years old next month."

I was trying to comprehend all of this when Helen stood up and tapped on her phone, and we heard a soft release of air coming from the side of Max's bay.

"C'mon, Max!" Helen said.

Max's ears perked, and he ran toward the tunnel along the side of his bay, disappearing for a moment before bounding toward us on the outside, oversized paws slapping the metal floor, tongue out, happily panting.

"Time to get going," Helen said as she reached down and gave Max a good scritch behind his ears. She lifted a leash off the side of the security scanner and placed it around Max's neck. He bit at it playfully, practically bursting with youthful exuberance.

"These guys will be fine until we get back," Helen said, waving her arm toward the enclosures behind us. "The automatic feeders will set in after about six hours and that should keep things going for several days. Can't say it will smell better when we return, but we need to make a visit to Basking's brother, Bernard."

CHAPTER NINE

Despite the heated floor, Dr. Albert Basking shivered in full-body convulsions. He stared straight ahead, eyes stinging from the blood that now coated them. The mirror reflected something he didn't recognize: a form, somewhat human-shaped, crumpled and limp, its once-muscular physique now a thin, blood-soaked mass. His expression an hour ago had been the epitome of practiced confidence and smug assurance, but it was now a grotesque canvas of pain and fear. Every breath was a battle, each inhale a sharp stab of agony in his bruised ribs. The vibrant color of his eyes had dulled, now a lifeless gray. Strands of his hair, matted with blood and sweat, clung to his forehead.

Against every prayer and plea, his mind remained sharp and calculating. He wished it weren't so, yearning to fall numbly into unconsciousness. Yet he felt as if every neuron in his brain was firing at once. This flood of mental activity locked him into a state of hyper-vigilance where pain, sharp and unrelenting, was his constant companion, each sensation amplified by his keen awareness.

Yet amidst this bleak tableau of defeat, a flicker of resolve stirred within him. He glimpsed movement—a shadow looming over him. It was her, the two-headed woman. Her imposing figure, a stark contrast to his broken form, was a beacon of strength. As she approached, Dr. Basking's mind grasped at this lifeline, his will to live igniting the last embers of his strength. His lips, cracked and dry, parted as he tried to muster a whisper, but only a hoarse breath escaped. He moved his arm away from his body and, using every bit of his strength, reached his hand toward the glass. The woman simply watched, motionless for several seconds, then walked over to the curtained side of the room. She disappeared for a moment, then reappeared holding a metal chair by one of its legs. Dr. Basking watched as the woman approached the pod, then twisted her formidable body, the chair held out at the end of her reach. With explosive force, she swung the chair at the pod's glass surface.

Dr. Basking clenched his eyes shut as the resounding concussion reverberated. He looked up and saw a small crack where the chair had contacted the glass and immediately moved his arm back to his side. While his forearm passed before his eyes, he glimpsed yellowish beads of fat bubbling from what used to be intact tissue. He closed his eyes, and the woman took another swing at the glass; this impact increased the length and severity of the crack. There were several more explosive impacts, and then, finally, he heard the chair drop to the tile floor beyond. He opened his eyes to see the woman prying a large section of the glass away and then stepping into the pod. Salvation, in its most unlikely form, had come for him. He let out a shallow chuckle that he would have allowed himself a moment of weakness. *Weakness is for mortals*, he thought, *not for gods*.

CHAPTER TEN

W e drove out of the parking garage—Helen next to me and Max sitting in the back seat. "So, what's the grand plan?" I asked.

"Save as many experiments as possible from Basking's office here and Bernard's lair where we're headed and get the hell out of Dodge . . . I don't know." She looked straight ahead as we moved into the waning light of evening, heading east. "I have no end game at this point. I just know that captivity, especially at the hands of Basking and his brother, isn't a life for any of them. Maybe it's time for the world to see them, for science to get access to the doctors' secrets. I just don't know."

"It's too bad we couldn't transport the experiments somewhere safe," I said.

I glanced at Basking's medical building as we drove by the front of it. The last light of the sunset reflected off the mirrored exterior, giving it an eerie, almost ethereal glow. Intended to be a bastion of trust and healing, the complex now seemed like a monstrous silhouette against the darkening sky, its secrets hidden behind a facade of shimmering glass. The main building and attached parking structure looked perfectly normal. The design that went into disguising the vast chambers within left me awestruck.

"I still can't believe those huge spaces are carved out of such a mundane-looking office building," I said. I saw a flash of movement in the back seat and glanced in the rearview to see Max looking out his window, too, as if tracking my statement with great interest.

Helen looked back at Max, too, and reached back to give him a scratch under his chin. "Rumor has it he used a couple of the engineers who had a hand in designing Disneyland. Ya know, the way the park hides the mechanics of their attractions so all you're left with is what they want you to see?"

"Oh, I know . . ." I said. "The engineers must have been pretty old, though. Disneyland opened in the 1950s, right?"

Helen turned to look out the front windshield. "Old or reanimated. That's Bernard's specialty. Keep going straight on Katella until you hit Beach Boulevard, then make a right."

We pulled up to a stoplight, and I faced her. "Let's play a game. Let's see if you can go over three minutes without warping my sense of reality to where I have to relearn the way the world works, as if I'm starting from an infant stage each time."

"Sorry," Helen said, brushing a strand of hair from her face. "You're gonna have to be pliable, I'm afraid. We've barely scratched the surface." We started driving again and several seconds of welcome silence hung between us.

Helen turned toward me. "Look at it this way. Each new revelation primes you for the next. If I were to tell you while you were in the exam room a couple hours ago that there was a sex-addicted, talking British turtle two floors below us, there's no way you would have believed me. Now, knowing that he exists, you're not surprised to see a fire-breathing bear or a six-inch-high elephant."

"Saying I'm not surprised is a bit of a stretch, but I catch your drift. Reanimation, though . . . That's next level. I mean, to tap into the mind of a dead Disney engineer, you couldn't just dig him up decades after they'd passed; you need to get to it before the brain and body deteriorate, which would mean Basking had to have the technology to reanimate for a long time—decades. He had to get to the engineers right after they died." I shook my head a little. "Still processing all this. It helps to talk it out."

"You're right in many ways," Helen said. "And I don't know the whole story either, but as I mentioned earlier, Basking's entire enterprise has been going on for much longer than most of us want to admit. Remember, there are notes I found going back 125 years—to 1899, to be exact. I have hundreds of pages on my phone, and I've been researching his life for over a year. I feel like I've been drawn into a vortex of secrets and sins. The more I read, the more disgusted I became, but also the more intrigued. Anyway, whether or not I wanted it, I've kinda become an expert on all things Basking."

"I'm all ears," I said.

Helen began unraveling a story that reshaped my understanding of my own past and brought forth some serious doubts about humanity's future.

"Way before this current generation of Albert and Bernard, there were the parents and the grandparents. I don't know how widespread this thing is, but I even found notes written by Albert's uncles and cousins."

"Thanksgivings must have been a hoot!" I interjected. "Bunch of mad scientists trying to decide how long to cook a turkey-pig."

"Basking's grandparents were instrumental in the forced sterilizations that took place in California mental institutions in the early twentieth century."

"Eugenics," I said.

"Yes, and . . ." Helen said as she flipped through more photos of the notebooks. "After California, the grandparents flew to Puerto Rico in the 1930s to help spearhead the mass sterilization of Puerto Rican women as part of their governor's so-called battle against poverty, but everyone knew he was secretly working with Hitler to keep the Aryan blood pool free from Latino blood."

"Jesus," I said.

"Then *their* kids, Albert and Bernard's parents, continued this family tradition." Helen flipped through a few more photos. "Here's a journal entry from Basking's parents dated August 2nd, 1973: 'Off to a great start. We've been able to replace many tribal doctors with our own and increase procedures by thirty percent in just four months.' They were part of the Native American sterilization procedures." She flipped to another photo. "Here . . . listen to this newspaper article from October 1977. 'Up to fifty percent of Native American women were sterilized during the six years from 1970 to 1976—many without consent, as part of a modern, covert eugenics effort. Many sterilizations were performed during routine appendectomies or other surgeries and the women didn't realize it for several months. Doctors and scientists who took part in these procedures and backed the cause are being questioned, among them noted geneticists Carla and Frederick Basking.' Awful, right?"

"No wonder the doctor got into genetics," I said. "He

basically just joined the family business when he was old enough."

"Pretty much," Helen said. "So, around 1984, Carla and Frederick—that's the parents . . ."

"I'm following," I said. "Barely."

"So, Carla and Frederick discovered a way to *chemically* sterilize men and women using a super-concentrated hormonal disrupter they created from phthalates and polychlorinated biphenyls—PCBs, if you're familiar—a bunch of other chemicals I won't even try to pronounce, and a stabilizer to help it absorb quickly but release slowly in the bloodstream over a long period, like a super-extended time-released agent. Remember, this was long before genetic manipulation at the DNA level—three decades or more before CRISPR. They did trials with prisoners—private prisons again—and the results were, according to their notes, successful."

"So they no longer needed to perform surgeries," I said.

"Right," Helen said. "But they still needed to target the populations that they didn't want to have procreating—essentially, anyone with skin color other than white—so they created a trans-dermal cream that could be applied to the skin of people through a distribution system that was broad enough to lower their birth rates, country-wide. In the fall of 1985, just as they were perfecting the formula, Carla had a stroke of evil genius, and a plan was born to distribute their chemical."

Helen pointed toward the light up ahead. "Keep going straight; our turn is another mile or so."

"Gotcha," I said.

Helen continued. "The notes of their brainstorming sessions are creepy as hell. They considered spraying the chemical over poor neighborhoods, mailing free face cream samples laced with the chemicals, even bribing snack vendors at sports stadiums to inject it into drinks, but nothing guaranteed the type of coverage or the narrow window of time they were aiming for until Carla came up with the idea for a nationwide event that was bound to attract not just hundreds or thousands of people, but millions—all in a single afternoon."

Silence once again fell, deep and profound.

"This is where you're supposed to guess what event it was," Helen said.

"Oh," I said, flustered. "Umm . . . mid-eighties time frame, millions of people all at once . . . Something to do with people watching for the space shuttle flyover or Haley's Comet? No, not during the day . . . Or a Madonna concert? I don't know!"

"Ever hear of Hands Across America?" Helen asked.

"My parents have a picture in their den with them holding hands during that!" I said.

"Cool! Yeah, well, it was all a master plot to mass-sterilize an entire population of minorities," Helen said way too matter-of-factly.

"Thanks. Rewriting history like this is just so much fun!"

"Well, in all fairness, even the organizers didn't know about the plot, so maybe you don't have to rewrite too much," Helen said. "Okay, in case you don't know the origins, Hands Across America was an organized charity event held in May of 1986, and it brought more than five million people together to create a continuous human chain from coast to coast.

"We lived in Long Beach at the time," I said. "I guess it ended there?"

"Yes, and that's likely where the photo of your parents was taken. The idea was people would come outside at 3:00 p.m. Eastern on May 25th and hold hands for fifteen minutes. People could reserve a spot in line for a few bucks and that money went to charity. Most people just came out and joined the human chain without paying, so it didn't raise much money, but it did get millions outside to take part."

"Okay, and?" I said, but before Helen could respond, the wail of emergency vehicle sirens interrupted us. "I have to pull over. Lots of flashing lights behind us . . . lots and lots."

Helen glanced back and looked through the rear windshield. Max got up on his hind legs and looked out, too. More than a dozen police cars raced toward us. We pulled over and watched them pass at blazing speed.

"Wonder what happened," I said, pulling back into traffic as the cops disappeared in the distance.

"I'm just glad we're not the target," Helen said. "Okay, where was I? So, the Baskings had about six months to plan how to target people and use Hands Across America to be the distribution vector. They wanted to get their sterilization chemical to all targets on the same day so they could accurately track the results. Remember—they're crazy, but they're still scientists, so they're methodical as hell. Carla worked with her political connections, who in turn worked *their* celebrity connections to get the idea for a nationwide charity event into the ears of Ken Kragen and Harry Bellafonte—the chair and co-chair of USA for Africa . . ."

"The 'We Are the World' song!" I said.

"Yes!" Helen responded. "And also the public-facing foundation behind Hands Across America, but Kragen and Bellafonte did not know what the Baskings were doing. In that way, Carla and Frederick's plan was . . . masterful." She paused for a moment, and that word hung there, probably way too long.

"You seem to admire that," I said.

Helen thought for another couple of seconds. "I admire nothing about *what* they did, but I admit that weaving their plan into the event was pretty damn cunning. I'm allowed to have two conflicting thoughts running around in my head . . . I'm a genetic experiment, remember?"

"Oh, I remember alright," I said.

Helen continued. "Anyway, the Baskings set out to use the event as part of their evil plan, but their plan needed a vector, a way to distribute their chemical, so they created a hand sanitizer. Hand sanitizer didn't exist for home use in the form we have today—the stuff we use is a relatively new thing, but this was the same idea. It was made with diluted hand lotion and enough rubbing alcohol to kill germs. They manufactured thousands of bottles of the stuff. Half of the bottles had their sexual sterilization chemicals in them, and half didn't. They came up with a simple system: the hand sanitizer with the black caps would have the chemicals in it, and the ones with the white caps wouldn't. The idea was, on the day of the event, at each support station along the entire event route—I'm talking in every state and every county—people would offer the white-capped sanitizer to white people and the black-capped sanitizer to everyone else."

"Devious as hell," I remarked. "Exploiting a charity event for their white supremacist agenda."

"Devious as hell, but evil as hell, too," Helen said. "They employed three thousand people nationwide, prepping them in shopping center parking lots with the hand cream and instructions the night before the event. The volunteers were told the lie that creams with white caps were for white or European skin and black caps for 'everyone else' had special moisturizers formulated for darker skin colors. The Baskings emphasized the discrete distribution—white and non-white—but didn't go so far as to raise suspicions. Anyone who disagreed forfeited their two hundred dollars shift pay, which was to be paid after they returned their allotted bottles, empty or full, the day following the event.

"The next day, May 26th, literally millions of people stood outdoors, ready for the event. If you look at videos from that day, it was a real party atmosphere. The distributors smoothly circulated among the crowds, promoting the lotion as a health measure. They casually infiltrated gatherings and festivals, seamlessly integrating into the festivities. By the end of the day, they had dispensed seventy thousand lotion bottles, half laced with their chemicals. They estimated they gave the chemical sterilizer to just over two million individuals."

"So, what happened?" I asked. "How did they track the results?"

"This is where things got ugly," Helen said. "I'm happy

to report that the mid- to late eighties were a dark time for the Basking family."

More police sirens and flashing lights interrupted us. I pulled over again, and we watched as at least twenty police cars and a few ambulances raced by.

"Jesus, that's a lot of cops!" I said. "Okay, continue please."

Helen continued. "So, about a month goes by and suddenly there are news reports about an early summer respiratory virus going around, but it never bubbled to the top headlines, so most people weren't aware or they ignored it. Carla didn't ignore the reports, though, because she recognized a few of the towns mentioned correlated to the event route, so she dug a little deeper. She made some calls to her doctor contacts and saw a strange trend: hospital admissions showed that nearly one hundred percent of people admitted for this illness were Caucasian, regardless of the region. When pressed, the doctors she spoke with were dumbfounded. She started mapping the infections and saw a direct correlation between the Hands Across America route and the incidents of infection."

"But why Caucasian?" I asked. Max barked from the back seat as a car's headlights swept through my car's interior.

"Why indeed," Helen said. "The Baskings only had a few weeks for their clinical trials in the prison population and so this respiratory thing never showed up as a side effect. I mean, colds and flu swarm around prisons, anyway, so no one was probably keeping track. It turns out that a few of the chemicals used in the sterilization cream hampered our cells' ability to absorb and use oxygen. It caused symptoms that presented like acute pneumonia, but chest X-rays didn't reveal any problems with the lungs. Most people recovered after a week or so, and there were only a few fatalities. Over the next two weeks, there was no ignoring the pattern, and Carla convinced Frederick to help her figure out what went wrong. Turns out their lead chemist had sabotaged the entire operation. He had communicated to the manufacturing folks that the white-capped bottles must contain the sterilization chemical, not the black-capped ones. They didn't question his authority, as he was their point of contact, anyway. It was a simple switcheroo that highlighted many huge flaws and potential security breaches in their plan."

"So, did anyone end up sterile?" I asked. "Oh, wait . . . Oh God, I think I know the answer."

"Why, what happened?" Helen asked.

"My parents told me they tried for almost five years to have a baby around that time," I said. "They told me the doctors couldn't find any physical anomalies but said there were hormonal imbalances that they just couldn't correct for. The doctors told them it was likely permanent.

It was horrible. Their dreams were being crushed! My mom told me stories of all the hope, heart-wrenching worry, sleepless nights, doctor visits . . . Fuck! I'm an only child because of these fuckers!"

"I'm so sorry, Joe." Helen looked at me and put a hand on my shoulder. "The sterilization attempt worked in about a quarter of the people who used the hand cream, but there were never any infertility patterns noted outside of the Baskings' research. The Baskings kept track, of course. Knowing what to look for, they monitored infertility rates along the routes through their contacts in the medical world, trade journals, whatever." She paused. "The effects weren't permanent, as you know, but they did last for several years in some cases."

"My mom told me they gave themselves five years to try, then decided to live their life as normally as possible. It almost broke them up. After seven years, I was . . . Well, I was a hell of a surprise."

Helen gave my shoulder a squeeze. "I'm glad you were. Albert and Bernard's older brother, Herbert, and his wife weren't so lucky."

"There was an older brother?"

"The favorite child, yes. Carla doted on him. They all did in their own way. He was a genius, handsome, and successful in his own work within their organization. He kept two bottles of the white-capped hand cream. His family used the cream all the time, like some people today use hand sanitizer. Because of their increased exposure to the chemicals, within just two weeks of Hands Across America, Herbert, his wife Florence, and his two young children all succumbed to the respiratory side effects and died."

"Jesus," I said. "I'm not sure how to feel about the parents, knowing how evil that family was, but the children . . . That's horrible."

"And it's probably what led Albert and Bernard to burn their parents' house down," Helen said. "That was in 1986."

I was silent for a minute or more. The evening turned to night. I thought about how I could have had brothers or sisters, about my parents' grief, about the pure evil that exists in this world.

More flashing lights appeared behind us.

"Pull over there," Helen said, pointing to a strip mall parking lot. "Look at that!"

A group of people moved about in front of a gas station on the corner, a half block ahead.

"Let's get out and walk, see what's happening," I said. Helen and Max turned toward me and Max let out a single "boof!" We got out of the car and then Helen pointed at the crowd.

"Oh shit!" she said. "That's Peter! Looks like he's in a fight!"

"Who's Peter?" I asked.

"The guy with the tail."

No more description was necessary. Who could forget Peter? Even from this distance, we could see his tail swinging about in a controlled, skillful manner as he swept it in a circle, fending people off. More people ran over and gathered near the corner. Police and other emergency vehicles swarmed the area. Whatever this was, it was growing in intensity and probably had no chance of ending well.

CHAPTER ELEVEN

T he three of us started walking toward the side-walk from the parking lot just as someone ran past on the street at a tremendous speed, her three arms pumping in furious rhythm and surprising grace.

"Debbie!" Helen yelled. "Oh no, this is going to get worse before it gets better. She's as strong as three men!"

The scene ahead of us was nuts. Dozens of people were now gathered in front of a lawnmower repair shop and a gas station on the corner. People were spilling out into the street, blocking the intersection. Max barked as another five or six police cars screamed past, lights flashing.

"I knew introducing these people into society would be a problem, but I didn't expect it to erupt into violence like this," Helen said. "At least not so quickly."

"Where's Peter?" I asked as we hurried up the

sidewalk, Max trotting along beside us, gripping his own leash in his teeth.

"There!" Helen said, pointing toward the parking lot ahead. We moved closer.

Peter was standing on the hood of an SUV, his tail poised like a viper, ready to use on anyone who stepped close. The muscular control he wielded was impressive. The tail was obviously as much a part of him as any other appendage, yet far more lethal.

"Stay back!" Peter yelled at the mob surrounding him. "I don't want to hurt anyone! I just want to get out of here!"

"You should have thought about that before you stole from my store!" yelled a man standing in front of the vehicle. He was wearing a shirt with an AM/PM convenience store logo on it. "And what the hell are you, anyway?"

"I only stole two candy bars!" Peter yelled, biting off a chunk of a Snickers and chewing frantically.

"Shit!" Helen exclaimed. "That's my fault. I forgot to tell them there was food in the kitchen refrigerators!"

"Well, freak?" the store manager yelled.

Peter glanced around for a way out, but as the term resonated with him, he steeled his eyes on the manager. "What did you call me?" he said and took a stride toward the manager, then leaped into the air. He twisted his body and slapped his tail down hard on the top of the man's head. The man crumpled to the ground and Peter jumped back onto the hood. The crowd squeezed in around the SUV, their angry voices splitting the night air with accusations and threats.

"You're a monster!" a woman screeched, her voice trembling with fear and anger. She had just exited the convenience store with her daughter, whom she clutched closer. She backed away with her child, her eyes never leaving Peter's tail.

Peter's gaze swept over the crowd, his eyes wide with fear. The situation was spiraling out of control, and every second that ticked by, his options dwindled. "Listen to me!" he shouted, trying to rise above the cacophony. "I'm not here to hurt anyone!"

But his words fell on deaf ears. The crowd's fear had morphed into a collective rage, a dangerous entity of its own. A bottle flew from the rear of the crowd, shattering against the SUV's windshield, splashing Peter with shards of glass and liquid.

More cop cars screeched to a halt as officers exited their vehicles and secured their batons and firearms, advancing toward the melee. One cop stood behind his open car door. He brought a bullhorn up to his mouth. "This is the Stanton Police Department. We declare this to be an unlawful assembly. I order all those here to disperse immediately. If you do not . . ." Before he could finish his sentence, there was a flash of green and his bullhorn was knocked from his grip. As the cop looked up from his now-empty hand, he saw a three-armed woman dashing away into the crowd toward Peter.

We were close now, standing at the periphery, but the crowd was huge, and it was getting harder to see what was happening. "We need to get higher so we can see," I said.

Helen and I looked around to see if there were any spots that offered a better vantage point. "How about that camper?" I said, yelling above the noise and pointing across the parking lot to an RV parked in front of the mower repair shop.

Without responding, Helen and Max ran toward the camper, and I followed.

A surge of voices and a few screams came from the crowd, and I looked over to see Debbie taking a running jump at a big guy who had climbed up on the rear bumper of the SUV and was coming up on Peter from behind with a baseball bat. She leaped into the air, turned her body nearly parallel to the pavement, and flew over the mob. She connected with the big man, firmly planting her feet on his chest. The man went flying into a car windshield, some twenty feet away, leaving him dazed but looking oddly at ease as he lay cradled in the web of fractured safety glass.

"Climb up. I'll hand Max to you," I said to Helen as

we reached the rear of the RV. As if he understood, Max jumped into my arms, and I handed him up to Helen. I climbed up the ladder and the three of us took our stance, with Helen and I crouching down to one knee to not be too conspicuous. Max sat between us, taking in the scene below.

By this time, between the public and the cops, there were probably one hundred people scrambling about. Peter and Debbie had dashed to safety after she dispatched the guy with the baseball bat but now had their hands full, facing off with a dozen guys who had them cornered near the gas pumps. One man, a real loudmouth who we figured to be the leader of that group, kept taking swings at Peter with a two-by-four.

"I ain't got no beef with you, lady," the man said, addressing Debbie. "But this freak is gonna pay!"

Debbie turned her attention to him, took a broad step in his direction, spun, and whacked the guy in the jaw with a butterfly kick. "Let's see how you feel about me now!" Debbie said. The man pirouetted into the gas pump and collapsed to the concrete.

Police were closing in and using their batons as they attempted to subdue the rioters. The guys surrounding Peter and Debbie scattered, moving back to the middle of the intersection, where another fight had broken out between some cops and the locals.

A few seconds passed, and we looked around for Debbie, finally finding her directly behind us on the repair shop roof. She was crouched, like Helen and me, but doing a far superior superhero pose with her two left arms extended in front of her at head level, eyes glaring forward. She arched her back, ready to release hell in a heartbeat.

"Debbie is badass!" I said.

"No shit! She was a flight attendant for nine years and a professional gymnast before that," Helen said.

A police helicopter sliced through the night sky, shining its spotlight onto the scene below.

It was about then that we heard the first shouts coming from a large crowd of people rushing toward the corner from across the street. Judging by the number of leather jackets and bandanas, word of the mayhem had reached Rusty's, the biker bar just up the boulevard. Most of the pack, armed with pool cues or knives, was led by a beer-bellied man waving his cap and shouting at the crowd.

"Damn," I said. "Those bikers will tear him apart!"

From somewhere near the front of the primary group of cops, there was a loud *pop!* and we watched as a smoke bomb canister arced its way into the center of the growing throng. People at ground zero followed its trajectory and dashed to safety. Another *pop!* and a canister I presumed to be tear gas, as it wasn't trailing smoke, flew through the sky. Out of nowhere, Peter landed directly under the incoming gas bomb and pivoted, cocking his tail back like he was ready to hit a home run. But instead of knocking it back into the group of cops, he shifted, aiming for the main group of aggressors who were forming in front of the gas station. As the canister came within tail's reach, Peter whipped his tail and made contact, propelling the cylinder high above the crowd and smacking the loudmouth leader of the main group directly in the forehead. The man released his two-by-four and flew back several feet onto his ass, then collapsed flat on his back.

There were three more smoke bomb launches from the police front lines, and Peter managed to divert two of them, knocking them a safe distance from the crowds, but the third one landed, spun past him, and came to a rest a few feet away. Peter leaped from his spot, and it was then that I could see that he used his tail like a third, powerful leg to help propel him as he jumped. He covered fifteen feet or more in one bound and came up right in front of the rest of the mob marching over from Rusty's. Peter looked behind him as if he himself was surprised at how far he could jump.

"Hey, freak!" one biker yelled, pointing at Peter and raising a pool cue into the air. "We got you!"

"Shit!" I said. "Now he's got to take on a biker gang, too?"

"No, wait!" Helen exclaimed. "Look!"

To my surprise, the bikers took a protective stance around Peter, blocking the aggressive crowd, forming a barrier between him and the angry mob. The helicopter light shone brightly on the scene, turning night into day.

"You want him, you'll have to get through us!" yelled the lead biker. The crowd continued advancing, pushing against the new protective circle. Leaping off the building roof, Debbie landed in the parking lot and rolled into an all-out sprint in one fluid motion. She elbowed and kneed her way through the mass and stood alongside her new allies, ready to protect Peter.

"Shit's getting serious," I said.

As the SWAT vans' rear doors swung open, ten well-armored team members from each van hopped out, helmets on and riot shields up, ready for action. We saw more civilians running toward the mass from every direction. Meanwhile, Peter and the bikers were fully surrounded and waves of people—civilians and cops—were moving in.

There was a crash and the sound of breaking glass just to our right. We turned to see that someone had thrown a rock or brick through the front window of the repair shop. The dull ringing of an alarm bell added to the cacophony.

"Looters!" Helen said. As we watched, two men emerged from the shop carrying various items.

"I think they're just gathering weapons," I said as we saw one of the men, a little guy no taller than five feet, pull the ripcord on an oversized chainsaw and hold the tool as it roared to life. He wielded the saw high above his head, lost his balance, and went crashing down onto the hood of a Tesla. We heard a horrible grinding noise as the saw bit into the metal.

The man scrambled to his feet, still holding the chainsaw, and yelled toward the crowd, "Hold him down! I'll take care of that tail!" Then he ran off, off-balance and zigzagging wildly toward the circle of people surrounding Peter.

"This is ridiculous. We've got to do something!" I said. "Where's Debbie?"

Helen and I looked around the scene but couldn't spot her. Several more men ran into the mower shop and came out holding metal rakes and shovels. One person had put on a pair of gloves and was swinging a gas-powered weed whacker.

"Not much of a weapon, but he gets points for creativity," I said, pointing at the weed whacker guy.

Helen and I looked at each other when the man passed beneath us and ran in the opposite direction of the melee.

"Oh, that guy—he *is* looting!" I said.

"Told you!" Helen responded.

Two more men ran out of the shop wielding machetes.

The biker gang had given Peter a chance to rest for a few seconds, but the two people with rakes had made their way to the inner circle and one of them had snagged a biker with the sharp tines and brought him down, opening a hole in their human shield. The other person with a rake lunged forward, swinging it wildly, causing a ripple of panic among the bikers. In that moment of chaos, Peter regained his strength and sprang into action. He moved with an agility that defied his size, quickly positioning himself between the attackers and the bikers. With a swift, calculated move, he grabbed the rake from the nearest assailant, twisting it from his grasp and using the handle to smack three of the attackers in the head before they even realized what had hit them.

More smoke bombs landed near that crowd, but the people just shifted formation and moved further away. The crowd moved in a fluid, organic motion as it reacted to the acrid smoke, then reformed, shifting and convoluting around the intersection, a relentless tide of bodies and chaos.

Two more bikers fell as they were hit with shovels. The chainsaw belched a trail of gray smoke as it moved through the crowd. The short man swung the roaring tool recklessly as he ran, forging an easy path to Peter through the throng. Peter stood, facing Chainsaw Guy, his athletic, lithe form ready to spring into action, but as he assessed the situation, looking at the chainsaw, rakes, knives, and shovels that were now approaching, he must have decided that fleeing might be the best way to avoid getting torn to bits. He crouched, ready to leap, but just as he squatted, three men grabbed his tail as Chainsaw Guy ran around behind Peter and revved the saw, ready to bring it down on the appendage. Debbie, who was busy fighting the two guys with machetes, glanced in Peter's direction but couldn't escape her own battle without getting sliced to pieces.

Helen and I watched with helpless frustration. There was nothing we could do from where we stood, and making our way into the mayhem would be suicide. Right as the chainsaw was about to make contact at the base of Peter's tail, a furious roar emerged above the din of the madness. The hush that fell over the crowd was palpable, and as people turned their attention toward the roar's source, Peter had the opportunity he needed to pull hard, forcing the three men holding his tail to stumble forward. Realizing he'd miss his mark, Chainsaw Guy thrust the blade down anyway, and it contacted the tip of Peter's tail instead of the base, slicing off the last foot of his appendage. The end of the tail wiggled vigorously on the pavement. Chainsaw Guy dropped the saw and picked up the stub, waving it in the air and shouting, "That's right! The little guy did this, motherfuckers!"

Most people just looked at him, but a few cheered. Overall, the brutal amputation rattled the crowd, giving Peter a chance to escape, but before he leaped to safety, there was another roar, and this time Helen and I saw its source.

"It's Jaguarman!" I said.

"His name is Gilbert," Helen said.

"There's no way in hell I'm calling him Gilbert," I said.

With breathtaking speed, Jaguarman hit the outer periphery of the crowd and leaped, gracefully skimming the tops of heads, and landed in the center next to Peter, facing the assailant. Chainsaw Guy dropped the tail and hoisted the chainsaw, fiercely pulling on the ripcord to get it started. Jaguarman rose to his hind legs in a slow and graceful show of force and dominance. He smiled at Chainsaw Guy, who was still struggling to start the engine and showing signs of fatigue, cursing and sweating profusely. Jaguarman brought his right paw back, and in a blink, he unsheathed five razor-sharp claws, each over two inches long. Chainsaw guy's eyes bulged in horror as Jaguarman, in a single, powerful slice, severed the man's arm at the shoulder. The arm and chainsaw dropped to the ground as a single unit, his index finger still twitching on the trigger. The man stood, stunned, unable to believe what had just happened, even as he looked at the blood spurting from the mound of flesh at his shoulder. Peter swung his damaged tail at the man's ankles, sending him crashing down.

The crowd surrounding Peter and Jaguarman thinned, the mob realizing rakes and shovels were no match for whatever these two creatures could unleash. By this time, a dozen more cops had joined the fray, yielding batons and riot shields as they made their way toward the center. Jaguarman, Peter, and Debbie forced a path away from the crowd, running up the boulevard to safety.

"If Jaguarman escaped, does that mean the other animals in the containment room have, too?" I asked.

"Not necessarily," Helen said. "If he got out, it's probably because he was a locksmith before Albert got hold of him. My guess is that he could have escaped at any time and was just waiting for the right opportunity. Speaking of getting out of here, we've got a chance right now and I suggest we take it."

We stood, ready to climb down the ladder to safety, but ducked as two gunshots rang out on the periphery, followed by the rapid-fire percussion of automatic weapons. We turned to see a dozen men and women jogging our way in a line formation, dressed in camo clothing and armed to the teeth.

"Stanton has a militia?" I asked.

"I don't keep up on those things. Do you?" Helen said, but before I could answer, bursts of muzzle fire ignited

the street. Multiple rounds found the repair shop's unbro-
ken window, bringing it down in a cascade of shattered
glass. The rest punctured the aluminum sides of the RV.

"Get down!" I said as we collapsed to the RV roof, lying
flat on our stomachs. My right arm held Max down and
hugged him close between us. We stayed still for several
seconds but knew it was in vain. The militia had seen us
and were, no doubt, surrounding the RV this very second.

"Why are they coming for us?" I whispered.

"No idea. Maybe being stranded on an RV roof makes
us easy targets," Helen said.

There was a pop and static. Then a man with a
Southern twang spoke into a bullhorn.

"Helen?" the man said. "What the hell? Okay, Helen
Hives—give yourself up. We've got you surrounded. You
and your companions come down here with your arms up
and we won't harm you."

We could hear voices and movement directly below us,
but also the growing sounds of the crowd from the intersection as it made its way closer.

"That's not a militia," Helen whispered. "I recognize that voice; it's Bernard's lieutenant, Hank. That's
Basking's goon squad!"

"I never thought I'd ever be in a position to wish for a
militia," I said.

"Basking's headquarters is just around the corner, but why would they get involved in something like this?"

I stared into the distance for a second, trying to concentrate. "Maybe they got word that a guy with a tail, a three-armed woman, and another guy with claws and fangs were fighting nearby," I said, looking at Helen. "That's hardly an everyday occurrence, and Bernard would know there was only one way that could happen."

"Sounds about right," Helen said. "Keep down!"

The goon squad had surrounded the RV. Loud, angry voices were closing in from all directions as the rest of the mob headed toward us. We realized there was no way down, and we were too far from the shop roofs to jump. We hunkered down, bringing Max in tight between us.

Hank's bullhorn crackled to life. "You've got ten seconds to come down or we'll come up there and get you. Trust me, you don't want that. Ten . . ."

"Shit, shit shit!" Helen said, terrified. Max nuzzled against her cheek.

"Nine." The parking lot was now full of people, their anger mixed with curiosity.

"Eight." The police spotlight now shone directly on the RV, the helicopter hovering close.

"Seven." Helen grabbed onto me tighter, the two of us lying flat on our stomachs, arms around each other. I could feel Max being squeezed out. He moved around to my other side.

"Six." Two more gunshots rang out, and we could hear even more sirens approaching.

"Five." The RV shifted as steel-toed boots clanged and clambered up the aluminum ladder.

"Four." My heart was beating in my throat. Helen's grip became tighter. Her fingers dug into my side.

"Three." A wave of hopelessness rolled through me. I turned and pressed my face against Helen's.

Silence.

The bullhorn hiss cut out, and there was a prolonged, eerie pause in the countdown. I held my breath for about ten seconds, but no "two" was spoken. Helen and I exchanged looks, eyebrows raised. I mouthed, *What the fuck?* And Helen shrugged.

There was a cracking and the hiss from the bullhorn returned but lingered for several seconds. Then, a throat clearing. "I'm sorry, folks," Hank said in a subdued tone.

Helen and I remained frozen. We could hear Hank's breathing, amplified through the horn. The helicopter rose, increasing altitude but keeping the light on us. The sound of the crowd had died down, too, with only the chatter of police radios and murmuring voices remaining. A few seconds passed. Then Hank spoke again. "C'mon, team, let's head out." There was a shuffling of boots and more murmuring voices. The bullhorn crackled. "Helen, I hope you'll find it in your heart to forgive me," Hank said, stuttering a little, his voice filled with emotion.

"Is he crying?" I asked Helen. She shrugged again and raised her head. We both got to our knees and peered over the edge. Sure enough, we saw big Hank wipe his cheek with the back of his glove as he turned, waving his team on to follow him. The rest of the crowd was already dispersed, heading out of the parking lot and walking off in all directions. Three cops hoisted a wounded officer onto a stretcher and helped him into the ambulance, but we saw no arrests.

"What the hell happened?" I asked but realized the answer as soon as I looked down at Max. "Hey, boy," I said to him. He turned his attention away from the crowd and looked at me, his natural smile greeting us, tongue out, a drop of drool hitting the roof.

"Amazing," Helen said, the two of us now standing, observing the scene. "I had no idea he could control the emotions of so many people at one time." Max wagged his tail, looking down at the aftermath below. "You're a *very* good dog!"

"Maybe he didn't control everyone's emotions," I said. "Maybe he just singled out the most aggressive person in each group, calmed them down. What if it just cascaded through the crowd?" I was theorizing, but it didn't matter in the end. The fact is that the scene went from explosive to peaceful in under a minute.

Headlights swept across us as cop cars and the SWAT vans backed away as if nothing had ever occurred here. Helen, Max, and I made our way down the ladder. I held Max as we walked through broken glass and debris and headed toward the car. The helicopter reeled off in a graceful arc, its spotlight turning off as it flew away.

—

We climbed into my car and drove through the now-empty intersection, turning right on Beach and traveling another couple of blocks.

"Park in that liquor store parking lot," Helen said, pointing to a neon sign.

I pulled into the Liquor Locker parking lot next to the Griffin's Nest Motel and parked.

We sat in silence for a few seconds, the experience of the street brawl settling in.

"I don't feel like flipping out anymore," I said to Helen. "I feel like I've already flipped out, and this is what being insane must feel like."

"I need your strength, Joe. Now more than ever. Now that Hank and the goon squad know I'm involved, they'll likely prepare for me at Bernard's lair."

"You've met Hank before?"

"A couple of times. The doctor used to meet with him in the office and we talked a little."

"I'm with you all the way, and I'll stay strong. As strong as a crazy person can be, that is."

"I guess that'll be good enough." Helen gave me a thin smile. "Okay, let me wrap up the Basking history lesson before we get to the next phase of my plan. The source of the house fire that killed Carla and Frederick was reported as bad wiring, but Albert and Bernard were responsible— they described their plan in another notebook I found a few months back right in there." Helen pointed at the Griffin's Nest Motel. "Don't get me wrong, the brothers are as evil as they come, but it looks like they changed direction from the eugenics-based plan that their parents and grandparents took."

"Yeah, they're not interested in a white-only race, just playing God to satisfy their own selfish, fanciful whims," I said.

"You're right, but it goes much deeper," Helen said. "The boys were in their mid-twenties when their family house caught fire. There were no formal inquiries, no signs of arson. Albert and Bernard eventually inherited their parents' estate, and that funded their enterprises to get them off the ground."

I was contemplating all that when Helen made a kissing sound, and Max bounded into the front and clambered onto her lap.

"Time to deal with Bernard," she said. Max's tail couldn't have wagged any faster.

CHAPTER TWELVE

Excruciating. That word above all others was at the center of Albert's thoughts as he lay in the back seat of the car. Albert enjoyed dissecting things, even words, and "excruciating" was his new favorite. Not only was it five syllables long, but it was also a challenge to say. It required an agile tongue, something Albert no longer had. Even to think through the word, to work through its distinctive phonemes, it required concentration and discipline. In fact, Albert thought as he tried to push the pain out of his throbbing head, the amount of mental gymnastics it took to articulate the word was, in itself, excruciating.

He smiled just a little at that thought, and the corners of his mouth creased and cracked and bled. He sucked in the blood with a quick inhalation and a swipe of what was left of his tongue. Another tooth dislodged, sliding deep into his mouth and nearly choking him. He tried spitting the tooth out, but that proved too painful, so he let it rest against his cheek with the others.

Under Albert's very slow and nearly unintelligible direction, the two-headed woman, whose real name was Arlene, had managed to wrap him up in a curtain from the display room and carry him to his car. She was surprised at how light he was, but as she picked him up, she saw the remnants of much of his mass on the pod floor. The pool of blood, fat, and subcutaneous tissue that probably constituted half his weight lay as a pink and yellow pool of organic detritus, already starting to stink from decay. She retrieved his keys from his blood-soaked pants, which had fallen off as his body shrank and shriveled from the advancing disease. Once at the car, she placed Albert into the back seat, then retrieved a towel from the trunk and draped it over her lifeless head to not draw too much attention from other drivers. She started the car, but before putting it into gear, she turned to Albert.

"I need your word that you'll make your brother fix me before he fixes you," Arlene said.

Albert's head stuck out from the curtain and he turned it to meet Arlene's eyes. "Yeshp," he gurgled.

That would have to be enough, Arlene decided as she began the drive to Bernard's lair.

PART THREE

June 7, 1968

California took the lead. Mandatory sterilization laws for the mentally ill, the criminals, the undesirables. A bold step. A triumph of reason over sentimentality. We must not waver. Even as the media and left-wing groups rail against the program. Those bleeding-heart liberals, they fail to grasp the magnitude of the problem. They cling to outdated notions of morality, blind to the scientific realities. They will learn. The future belongs to the strong, the intelligent, the pure. We are the architects of that future. We are doing God's work.

The Journal of Frederick and Carla Basking

PART THREE

CHAPTER THIRTEEN

I 'd always wondered why there were so many small, low-rate motels along this strip of Beach Boulevard. There was the prostitution trade, but could that support all of these motels sitting on expensive Southern California real estate? The motels certainly didn't appeal to tourists—they were all too far to walk to Disneyland or Knott's Berry Farm, and their overall appearance and amenities didn't make them attractive to families. *Free Wi-Fi, Cable TV!* Big deal. Yet there they were, over two dozen motels along a three-mile strip. Many offered weekly rates, so people were likely using them as housing; perhaps that explained it. I don't know—it's a mystery.

Helen, in the short time I'd known her, had offered more questions than answers. Most shook my very perception of reality, but it wasn't her fault. My reality could use a little shaking up, I suppose. When I posed the question of these motels, however, she had one very simple explanation.

"A few are still privately owned, but Basking Enterprises owns about fifteen of them," she said, pointing to a few of the properties around us as we advanced on the Griffin's Nest Motel.

"The Covered Wagon Motel is about two blocks up the road." Helen pointed behind us. "Basking doesn't own that one, at least, not yet. My family had to stay there for almost six months back in the late nineties after my dad got laid off. I didn't mind it, but I was like seven years old, so what did I know? I stayed there again for two nights just about a month ago, wanting to make sure it was still safe enough for our friends. The owner's son now owns the property. I remembered him from our stay there twenty-five years ago—we were the same age, so we caught up. I didn't give him any details, just asked that he reserve ten rooms for a month for a few unusual guests. He didn't ask questions and happily obliged. I'm guessing that's where Debbie, Peter, and Gilber . . . um, Jaguarman are now."

"Is it safe to have them stay this close to Bernard's lair?" I asked.

"They need to be close," Helen responded. "I don't know how they'll react to being out of their pods for the first time. If they end up needing something medically, I can likely find it at Bernard's."

"Is there a chance some of their genetic mutations could be reversed?" I asked.

Helen slowed her pace as if the question had stumped her, then stopped and turned to me. "It's complicated. Thing is, not all of them want to change back. That's not to say they don't miss their old lives. It's just that after you've been altered, you grow into the new being you've become. I've been working with them over the past year, helping them embrace and celebrate the new, improved versions of themselves rather than denying them. As much as I hate Basking, I've learned to love the new me. I'm pretty sure that's the case with the others as well." She hesitated for a moment. "Then again, life outside the pods is a whole new ball game."

"I get it," I said.

"It's okay, normie," Helen said, smiling.

"Ha! Yeah . . . I kind of envy you guys, actually. What I've seen tonight has impressed the hell out of me." We started walking again.

"All this applies to the people in the display room— the museum. The creatures in the containment room . . . Well, I have a tentative plan about what to do with them, but it's going to take some work. It's a complicated situation, for sure."

"Can we slow down a little?" I asked. "My leg is killing me."

"Sure thing, but let's get around to the back of this place first, if possible," Helen said. "Shit, we need to change your dressing, too. Remind me once we get—"

SLAM!

The sudden force knocked me onto the asphalt. I rolled until I came to a stop against the motel wall. I could hear Max yelping close by, and when I opened my eyes, I saw Helen was on the ground, too, struggling to stand. Max was being stuffed into a bag by two . . . What the hell were these things? Hairless gorillas came to mind. It's important to clarify here that I'm talking about literal gorillas, not goons, thugs, or hooligans. *God*, I wish I was! But in this new reality, of *course* they would be some kind of human-gorilla hybrid. Both were wearing board shorts, and the smaller of the two had a mohawk . . . Okay, that kind of surprised me.

Helen caught my eye as she got to her feet. "Run!" she yelled.

I didn't need that direction, but it was nice knowing we were both on the same page. I got up, painfully extending my wounded leg, and glanced over at the gorillas who were struggling with getting Max into the bag, which was a little too small for him. He was all paws and legs, and under any other circumstance, the sight of the gorillas struggling to gently stuff him into the cloth bag would have been hilarious. By the time I turned back to Helen, she was dashing ahead; I followed.

I was just behind Helen as she rounded the corner and nearly ran into her as she skidded to a stop, her arms swinging wide, trying to catch her balance. Just ahead, six more gorillas came at us, this time with nylon nets. Helen made a break for it and leaped a dozen feet over some trash barrels, grabbing the bottom rung of a fire escape ladder. She clambered up, swinging herself up to get a foothold, but one gorilla jumped after her and grabbed her ankle. They both crashed down atop the barrels, scattering trash and finally hitting the pavement. Two nets were thrown, and the gorillas surrounded us. The more we fought, the more tangled we got. I gave up fairly quickly, not wanting to damage my leg any further. Helen was demonstrating amazing strength—much more than I knew she had. After I stopped fighting, the gorilla behind me zip-tied my wrists and took the net off. I stood there watching in amazement as Helen fought off four gorillas at once from inside her net. At one point, she looked over at me and resigned, bringing her hands down and clasping them behind her.

I heard a muffled yelp and looked over to see the gorilla with the mohawk holding the bag with Max in it. He and his partner were coming up beside us. "Got dog," Mohawk said. Two others grunted in response. "Take prisoners now!" he commanded. "Must get them to doc-tor."

The gorilla closest to me turned and looked quizzically at Mohawk. "Why are you talking like that, dude?" he asked in a distinct surfer accent.

Mohawk laughed, bringing his hand up to his mouth, chortling around it. "Just messin' with them."

"Well, mess with them on your own time, dickhead. We've got work to do."

Helen, Max, and I were escorted behind the motel to a building that looked like a standalone garage. We walked through the nondescript door and into an elevator. I was surprised to hear Muzak playing as the doors closed. "Raindrops Keep Falling on My Head" emerged from the ceiling speaker.

"Man, I'm tired of this song," Mohawk said, which made me wonder if they just kept it on a loop for this elevator—a demented but appropriate soundtrack for guests making the descent into the unknown.

The ride lasted close to a minute, dropping us deep underground. There were no buttons. No displays. Just the sensation of falling, perhaps a hundred feet or more. Stepping out, we entered a corridor. It was sleek, with polished surfaces and a futuristic vibe. From there, we walked into a large room that had all the trimmings of a well-equipped, state-of-the-art laboratory, complete with bubbling test tubes, hissing gas lines, and even a Jacob's Ladder, which crackled with electricity, casting an eerie glow over the metal surfaces. Rows of sleek, stainless-steel tables lined the space, each one cluttered with an array of scientific paraphernalia: microscopes, Petri dishes teeming with colorful specimens, and displays blinking with data. The air was filled with a mix of chemical scents, sharp and antiseptic, overlaying a distinct scent of ozone, like the smell of rain evaporating off asphalt. Bright overhead LED lights illuminated the room, leaving no shadowy corners, making the laboratory feel both clinical and otherworldly. In the far corner, a man wearing a white lab coat stood at a workstation surrounded by monitors, each screen showing a different angle of the laboratory or zoomed in on microscopic images, revealing the minute details of his experiments.

Helen and I exchanged a look of awe and unease; this place was obviously the heart of the operation, a blend of cutting-edge technology and unsettling biological research. Being such, I realized there was no way that we would be allowed to bear witness to this place and leave here alive.

I turned to see the eight gorillas standing in a semicircle around us. Mohawk was closest to me and gave me a big grin when our eyes met. "Are we having a moment?" I asked.

His smile disappeared, and he looked down. "Shut up, no!" he said. Three of his buddies giggled.

"Dude, if you like him, it's okay," one of them said.

"Shut the fuck up!" Mohawk replied.

"Enough!" The voice came from the man wearing the lab coat. He turned away from the bank of displays and moved over to us in long strides. "Please excuse Kai and his buddies here. Seems you can put the gorilla into the human, but you just can't pull all the human out of the gorilla . . ." He hesitated and looked to the side for a moment, assessing his statement. "That didn't come out exactly as I had hoped. Anyway, my name is Bernard Basking, and allow me to introduce you to Kai, Bodie, Dax, Zach, Blaze, Maverick, and . . ." He nodded toward the smallest gorilla, the one at the end of the line holding the bag with Max in it. "What name shall we call you today?"

"Grinder," said the gorilla, wiping his nose with his other hand.

"It's Milton!" Mohawk said, grinning. "You can't give yourself a nickname. It doesn't work like that. No one ever called you Grinder, not even your skater buddies!"

"Shut up. They did too," Grinder said, showing his fangs.

"Now now, boys," Bernard said, waving his index finger at them. "And Milton, yes."

"Your names sound very familiar," I said, looking over the faces of the gorillas.

Mohawk spoke up. "If you followed big wave surfing at all in the past decade, you'd know us. Well, you'd know all of us except Milton. You'd know him if you had a subscription to *Dweeb Digest*." A chorus of laughs came from his buddies.

"That's right!" I said, snapping my fingers. "You all went missing a couple of years ago on your way to Portugal, I think. Your plane crashed—no survivors."

"Nazare, Portugal," Mohawk interjected. "Except our plane was hijacked before we crashed into the ocean and we were picked up by—"

"Yes, yes, yes." Bernard gave a dismissive wave of his hand. "No need to bore them with details. And it was a controlled water landing, not a crash. Anyway, enough with the formalities." He looked at Helen. "Helen Hives, I don't really know why you're here, but the fact that there was a street brawl involving a man with a tail, a woman with three arms, and a half-man, half-panther tells me—"

"He's a jaguar," I said. "Panthers are black-coated leopards."

"Okay, jaguar, sure, and what is your name?" Bernard pointed his chin at me.

"Joe," I said.

"Okay, Joe, anyway, piecing this together doesn't

exactly tax my genius. The question is, how did you pull this off? I have a call in to my brother, but Albert must be preoccupied."

There was a long silence as Bernard stared at Helen.

"I'm sorry. I lost track of the conversation," Helen said. "Are you waiting for one of us to talk?"

A blank look flashed over Bernard's face, and he blinked. "I . . . Forgive me, I don't really remember. But it doesn't matter. Until we get this figured out, I'm afraid you and your friend here are going to be my guests."

"What about Max?" I asked.

"Who in the blue blazes is Max?" Bernard chuffed out.

"Max is our dog. Grinder is holding him in the bag."

Bernard shot Grinder a look. Grinder smiled brightly, obviously pleased to hear his nickname used.

"If memory serves, Max is a special dog, isn't he? Albert was very proud of that one. He'll stay safe with us. Milton, give Bodie and Zach the bag—you two figure out a way of giving Max some water and food, but do *not* look at his eyes. The rest of you, show Helen and Joe to their room. If anyone needs me, I'll be in the crematory."

—

We were shuffled out of the lab and into a long hallway. We reached the end, where a set of double doors led into a large room filled with cages. There were other things in cages there, too, but they remained unseen, clinging to the shadows. Mohawk spoke up. "Milton, open number five and stay in here with them. You get first watch."

"But I haven't eaten dinner yet."

"We need to feed them, so we'll bring you something, too," Mohawk said.

Helen spoke up. "Please bring us a stack of four-by-four wound dressings, Aquaphor, and antibiotics—amoxicillin if you have it. Joe has a wounded leg."

Mohawk glanced at me and nodded while giving a deep grunt.

I was relieved to see there was a toilet in the corner of our cage and made a beeline for it. After I finished, I walked over to Helen, who was watching the other gorillas gathering around one of the cages near the opposite corner. They were vocalizing with something in the cage, but they weren't talking; they were chuffing and grunting. This lasted about a minute before Grinder broke off from the group and came toward us, finally settling on a chair facing us. The rest of the gorillas left the room. Helen and I looked at Grinder for a few seconds, his eyes meeting ours. Helen tugged gently on my arm, signaling me to walk with her. We turned and walked toward the far corner and sat on the metal bench.

"They didn't ask for our phones." Helen said.

"Whoa, you're right," I replied, feeling my pocket for my phone's outline.

Helen turned slightly, using my body to hide her actions as she slipped her phone out of her back pocket and looked at the screen. "No signal at all. Not even a network carrier icon."

"Must be why they didn't ask for them. This place is at least five stories below ground, and with all the metal around us, it's like being in a giant Faraday cage." I turned away from Grinder, some twenty feet from us, and glanced at my phone screen. Finding the same result, I noted my phone's battery at twenty-seven percent, then put it into battery-saver mode and put it back in my pocket. "Put your phone into power-saver mode. That way, it won't burn through the battery while constantly trying to access a signal."

"Smart," Helen said. "My phone is showing thirteen percent battery. I think I'll just turn mine off for now." She slipped her phone back into her pocket and looked at me. "Milt . . . Grinder isn't appreciated. He's an outcast and is looking for a connection."

"Do you want to talk with him and try to connect?" I asked.

"I think you should. He needs a male friend."

She was right, of course. Talking to a pretty girl might work well at first, but quickly Grinder would be reminded that a relationship with a human female while he was in his current form was impossible, and the frustration would likely cause him to withdraw. If there was any chance of Grinder helping us, I'd have to be the one to talk with him. I walked over to the front of the cage and rested my hands casually on the bars.

"Hey, Grinder," I said. He looked up at me but didn't meet my eyes. "I never surfed, only body-surfed and boogie-boarded, but I used to skateboard like crazy."

Grinder continued looking at the floor, his arms resting on his knees, hands clasped. I glanced back at Helen, who rotated her hand, giving me the "keep going" gesture, but Grinder spoke before I had the chance to turn back to him.

"Where'd skate?" he asked, looking up at me.

"Just around town," I said. "I grew up in Long Beach and the skater culture was pretty strong there. How about you?"

"Hermosa," Grinder said. "Mostly around town, but when I was twelve, they built a skate park a couple blocks from our apartment, so that was cool, I guess."

"Very cool. I've never skated in a park; always afraid I'd make a fool out of myself."

"Pretty common to be intimidated by them, but that kinda sucks, right? I mean, skate parks are for everyone, but most people don't feel comfortable going to them. That's one thing I'd change if I could build my own park."

"What other things would you do to make your park different?" I asked.

I worried that he would ignore my attempts at conversation but like many who are ignored by their peers, Grinder was grateful for anyone willing to listen. His face lit up as he told me his ideas, his words coming faster and freer the more he spoke.

"A lot of parks have areas for beginners, but I'd have an area for total newbies that has free lessons by some of the more advanced skaters. There would always be at least one experienced skater in the newbie section designated to help beginners—everything from choosing the right boards to learning basic skills and then gaining techniques as they get better. It would be a safe space for people of all levels, even those who have never skated before. We'd even have free board rentals for newbies so they can try out different ones to see what works best for them. As they advanced, they could be mentors for others who are just starting out. It would be organized but casual, with an emphasis on being fully inclusive—kids with disabilities, wheelchairs, everyone would be welcome."

"Wow," I said. "You really have given this some thought! What a fantastic idea!"

"Yeah, well," Grinder said as he broke eye contact and lowered his head, "doesn't hurt to dream, I guess, but it's pretty painful knowing it will never happen now."

I could hear the resignation in his voice, the turmoil.

I looked back at Helen. She stood up and walked toward me, stopping just short of the bars.

"I know what it's like to be an outcast," Helen said gently.

Grinder raised his head and looked at us. "Really? How's that? Being beautiful is somehow holding you back from living your dreams?"

Helen's voice carried a quiet strength as she responded to Grinder's skepticism. "It's easy to see the surface and make assumptions," she said, her gaze steady and unwavering. "But sometimes, what's hidden beneath can tell a deeper story."

Taking a step closer, Helen reached up to her face, her fingers tracing the contours of her jawline as if preparing to unveil a secret long kept. "You see me now, in this light, and you see what appears to be unblemished perfection," she continued, a hint of sadness threading through her words. "But this"—she gestured to herself—"isn't my reality."

With a deep breath, as though she was bracing herself for the vulnerability of her next act, her demeanor shifted. She closed her eyes and placed her hands on the bars. When she reopened her eyes, there was a resolve that hadn't been there before. Slowly, starting with her hands, she began to change. Her skin rippled like a calm pond stirred by a breeze. Previously flawless skin shifted in tone, becoming uneven and blotchy. Deep pockmarks, the scars from her cystic acne, appeared and crept up her arms, finally reaching her neck and face. The vibrant glow that once defined her dimmed as her pallor shifted and cooled. Her skin was no longer smooth but stratified and scarred, revealing a painful history of botched treatments and failed cures. As the last traces of Eve 19 vanished, Helen stood before us, somehow more powerful than before. Her eyes now told a story of the suffering, struggle, and resilience of a person who'd faced her deepest fears and emerged victorious.

The room was quiet for several long seconds. Helen stood there as we looked on, witnessing her in her true form, not as a beacon of perfection but as a symbol of courage.

Focusing her attention on Grinder, Helen continued. "Bernard's brother, Albert, tried for years to give all the Eves—the women like me—eternal beauty, but there is no such thing. I've learned to repress my true self, to hide what you see here, but it's exhausting." Helen clenched her eyes and stood there as if in deep concentration. Her skin changed again, but not back to its former perfection—rather, to a more normal appearance. Pockmarks were filled, and most scars disappeared. Now she wasn't perfect, but she was better. She was human.

Grinder stood and walked to within a few feet of our

cage. He looked deep into Helen's eyes—and there was a connection there that even I could feel. Something that transcended physical appearances and touched the core of their shared humanity. I, too, saw Helen in a new light, not just as a nurse with a mysterious past but as a warrior who had fought her battles and emerged with a deeper understanding of what it meant to be truly human.

CHAPTER FOURTEEN

There was a clatter as the door to the chamber swung open and three of the gorillas stepped in carrying metal trays.

"Chow time!" Zack said. "Open up the cage, Milton."

Grinder stood and walked over to Helen and me. We backed up and let him unlock the cage. Zach handed us the food trays, and Bodie handed us the tray with the wound dressing and antibiotics.

"Thanks," I said as Helen and I sat on the concrete floor and examined the food. Bodie glanced up at me and gave a soft grunt and a nod. Milton closed and locked the cage door as Dax set Grinder's food tray on his stool. Then all three left the room. Grinder went back over to his stool, where he picked up his food and dug in.

"Let's get this antibiotic into you first," Helen said, handing me a pill.

There was a commotion from the back, heavy grunting and movement.

"Grinder, what's back there?" I asked.

"That's Boris," Grinder said around a mouthful of food. "He's a real gorilla." He swallowed his food and motioned toward Boris's cage. "Boris was Albert's first attempt at creating a human-gorilla hybrid. He started with a gorilla and tried to blend in human DNA, but it didn't take. Gorillas are genetically ninety-eight percent human to begin with. Anyway, it made him smarter but not obedient or controllable. Plus, it didn't change his looks at all for whatever reason, so he's considered an NVH."

"Nonviable humanoid," I said.

"Right! Helen taught you well. Anyway, he hates that term, of course, because he's not human and therefore not a humanoid."

There was more commotion from behind us as Boris stirred and chuffed.

"Can you understand us, Boris?" I asked, turning my head toward him.

Grinder cut in. "He understands some but usually only communicates with me and the other gorillas."

"Doesn't he get to eat?" Helen asked.

"They feed him through the back of his cage. There's a door there that leads to another room behind that last row of cages. No one can get close to Boris—no human, anyway. One of Bernard's lab assistants, a real sadistic bastard named Scott, got within arm's reach of Boris's cage a couple months ago and Boris tore his arm off, then ate it."

"Oh my god, what happened to Scott? Did he die?" I asked.

"No, he's okay, unfortunately. No one really seems to die around here. They just get fixed or recycled. I heard that while he was in our medical bay, they gave him a new arm. They used one from a North Pacific giant octopus."

Helen and I looked at each other, and I swallowed a bite of my sandwich. "That's oddly specific," I said.

"I'm kinda a marine biology nut, so I dug deeper once I heard the term 'octopus.' The North Pacific giant octopus seemed like an odd choice because it's the largest species. His arm didn't need to be ten feet long. Turns out, Bernard added a layer of erectile tissue to the arm, so in its normal state, it's the right size, but when Scott wants to, he can make it, like, three times bigger." Grinder bit into a carrot stick, chewed while thinking, then swallowed. "From what Scott tells me, it's pretty cool, but every time he reaches for something, he gets a boner."

I nearly choked on my turkey sandwich. Helen chuckled around her hand. "How long have you been waiting to tell that joke to someone new?" I asked.

"*So* long!" Grinder responded, snickering. "Anyway,

Boris was never wild; he was in a Russian circus when Bernard found him. Story goes, he was taken from his troop in Rwanda when he was about a year old and flown to somewhere in Siberia to be part of a circus. No other gorillas around, but there were two chimps who kinda raised him, some other animals. Sad story, really. Bernard doesn't have extended plans for NVHs, so some end up here in this room."

"What else is in here?" I asked.

"I am," came a raspy voice from the shadows.

Helen and I squinted at the cage behind Grinder and could see movement. We both stood and moved to the bars for a closer look.

The figure stepping forward into the dim light was dressed in modern but slightly oversized clothes. His shoulder-length brown hair looked windblown, but it was his face that fascinated me. Deep-set dark eyes stood out from creased, leather-like skin, much of it covered in the thicket of his unkempt beard. He moved into the well-lit part of his cage and nodded. "Otzi," he said, smiling.

Helen and I exchanged a glance, the absurdity of the situation momentarily forgotten in our intrigue. "You're . . . Otzi? The Iceman?" I asked, my skepticism mingling with a growing sense of wonder. "We learned about you in my anthropology class."

"Yes," Otzi replied, his gaze steady. "Though I find

myself far from my Alpine resting place," He paused for a moment. "Alexa, turn on lights." His enclosure lit up with subtle amber lights, arranged for a dramatic, but tasteful affect. He gestured around the cage, which had been meticulously transformed to mimic a Copper Age hut. Animal skins layered the floor, and an electric fireplace with a built-in heater stood in the corner, simulating a traditional firepit. Above the firepit hung a display with a collection of the personal items found near his body: a bow and quiver with arrows, various arrowheads, a knife, and a small copper-bladed ax. Attached to the bars on the far wall was an enormous LED display.

"This was a nice touch," Otzi said, reaching into his pocket and producing a small remote. He turned the display on. Glowing to life was an expansive vista of green and reddish-brown rolling hills, the palette enriched by vast swathes of heather that painted the landscape in a spectrum of warm autumn hues. The sun shone through billowing clouds and reflected off patches of ice and water that dotted the landscape. As the scene shifted and panned, a roaring stream came into view, it's clear, glacier-fed water running over rocks and rushing toward a distant lake. It was a timeless panorama that one could have easily witnessed today or thousands of years ago.

"Bernard believes in comfort, or his version of it, at least," Otzi continued, a wry smile on his lips. "He's given me much more than I ever had." He gestured to his living space.

"They let you keep your weapons?" Helen asked.

"If you look closely, you'd see they are toys made to look like my belongings. My proper bow, arrows, and ax are in a climate-controlled room in some museum somewhere." Along the wall opposite the display, there were row after row of bookshelves, overfilled with volumes. "One of the first things Bernard did for me was teach me to read. That couldn't have been easy for him."

Helen moved closer to the edge of our cage; her eyes wide with fascination. "I remember seeing news reports when they found you, but you weren't alive; you were more or less mummified, frozen in the High Alps. You're, what, five thousand years old?"

Helen was doing a great job of remaining calm, but she was obviously amazed. This was the first time I'd seen her like this. She was finally seeing something that surprised her. That made me feel a little better. I no longer felt like the only one caught in an alternate universe.

Otzi chuckled, a sound that seemed to carry the weight of millennia. "Five thousand three hundred and ninety-two years old, but who's counting, eh? And yes, that's the marvel of modern science. Bernard has his methods. Methods that seem to defy both nature and ethics. Strangely, I don't have any regrets. I guess it's all a matter of perspective. Hunting and gathering isn't all it's cracked up to be." He looked at Grinder, who was listening to all this with rapt attention, apparently never having engaged with Otzi at this level before. Otzi smiled, then chuckled. "I'm not crazy about being caged up, but Bernard comes here nearly every night. He brings me books and we enjoy a brandy or cup of tea and talk for an hour or so before he goes off to bed. It's been almost thirty-five years since the hikers found me and about thirty since I was fully healed and ready to face the world, but . . ." He trailed off for a moment, then looked at us. "The, um, experiments in blending me into society weren't successful. I, uh . . ." He hesitated again. "I apparently don't play well with others." He looked away from us and down to his cage floor. "Something about my wiring, I guess. My evolutionary impulse control isn't up to today's standards. Let's just leave it at that."

"But scientists are still studying you," Helen said. "I read that, just recently, they sequenced your DNA. If you're here, then what body are they studying?"

"What body indeed," Otzi said. "Bernard showed me the same articles and I find it fascinating."

"So, you're there in a lab and here?" I said.

"Bernard mentioned something about cloning but lost me in the details. The Otzi they are studying, from my understanding, is my exact duplicate or I am his. In any case, from the photos I saw in the article of that dried-out carcass in the museum, I'm glad I'm the one talking with you today."

"So you're okay with this? Being . . . alive again?" I asked.

"There's not much choice in the matter," Otzi said, his expression sobering. "I find solitude suits me, but that doesn't mean I don't miss my family and my community."

"Do you remember anything from the reanimation process, or is that too sensitive of a subject?" I asked, eager to learn more.

"I remember the pain but not much else. From what I was told, it took over a year to bring me fully back to life, raising my body temperature by one degree every couple of weeks to discourage cell damage. They induced a coma and kept me in a lab, slowly re-nourishing me, essentially filling my emaciated corpse with life. I have no memories other than pain, but maybe that's a good thing. I don't really want or need to know the details of the process. Somewhere in there, they gave me new teeth, too. My wife had died, essentially of rotten teeth, as many people did back then. Take care of your teeth! That's my favorite bit of advice."

"I'm sorry you had to go through all that," Helen said.

"Seems like we've all been altered in some way, doesn't

it?" Otzi said. "I heard you and Grinder talking a few minutes ago. We all carry burdens, don't we?"

His question, like so many events of the day, caused me to reflect on how my experiences over the last several hours had profoundly altered my world views.

Without looking, I reached over to Helen and grabbed her hand and held it reassuringly.

Otzi smiled, his beautifully white teeth practically glowing. "I've learned much since awakening. The world has changed, but some things remain the same—greed, curiosity, the quest for power. But it's not all bad. Love still seems to be out there. Kindness. Generosity. Not everyone has these virtues, of course, but a lot, if the books I read can be trusted."

Behind us, Boris grunted, a reminder of our surreal surroundings. In that moment, Otzi's cage felt less like a prison and more like a bridge spanning the chasm of time, connecting us to a past we could only imagine. Here was a man—or, rather, the reanimated essence of one—who had walked the Earth in an era so remote it was nearly unfathomable.

"What do you want to do now?" Helen asked. "What does a 5400-year-old person want from this world?"

Otzi's gaze drifted toward the artificial horizon on the screen, which now displayed ice-capped peaks behind a perfectly still lake. "I'd love to go fishing again," he said, simply. "I've never fished for pleasure. It's always been for survival. I can only imagine how fun it might be to fish just for the thrill of the catch."

Grinder spoke up, his voice wavering a bit. "I don't know how I could help you with that, but if there's something else I could get you, let me know."

Otzi gave a quick chuckle and an appreciative smile. "Aside from new books, which Bernard brings me each week, I don't want much. Seems modern materialism isn't a concept that I've learned to embrace." His kind smile seemed to warm the spaces between us.

"Nothing at all?" Helen asked.

Otzi looked around him as he considered the question, his eyes coming to a stop on the display. "Netflix would be nice. These scenes are beautiful, but I don't need to be reminded of my homeland 24/7. I've always wanted to watch *Seinfeld*. Bernard says introducing too much modern society will create an imbalance and damage me somehow—hence the animal skins and such. I agreed at first, but now I don't know. I think I'm ready for it."

Grinder grinned. "I'll see what I can do."

"Hey, Grinder," I said, nodding in his direction. "Let's talk for a second."

Grinder seemed to ignore my request at first as he

finished up his dinner, but then he looked back up to Helen and me. "I know what you're going to ask me to do, but it's impossible."

"We're offering you a chance at freedom here," I said.

Grinder picked at his plate, not looking up, and was silent for a bit. "Look, you two seem like good people, but I can't help you escape. Think about it—I may not exactly fit in here, but I sure as hell wouldn't fit in on the outside." He waved his long, muscular arm about the room. "None of us would."

Helen looked at Grinder with kind eyes. "We understand, Grinder."

I moved closer to her ear. "We do? Is this how we're going to leave it?"

She tugged at my arm and the two of us walked back over to our food near the back of the cage. We sat, and she picked up her sandwich. "I'm not giving up, but Grinder is coming from a place of fear right now and I can't blame him. We'll need to consider a different angle if we want his help."

Helen nodded thoughtfully and returned to her food. Another minute or so passed.

"Not to change the subject, but I think you're still very pretty," I said.

She smiled a little. "Thank you."

"What you did was very brave. Peeling back the layers,

so to speak, and exposing yourself like this. You keep surprising me."

"You barely know me," she said.

"Doesn't mean I can't be surprised."

We ate in silence for a while. My eyes drifted to the large
display in Otzi's area. The panorama of a tundra dissolved
into an archipelago, a string of islands that looked familiar, but I couldn't quite place them. The drone footage was
detailed and well-produced, with crisp details providing a
mesmerizing video of the sea and the tawny landscape of
the islands. As the camera flew over the last island in the
chain, it tilted and a seaside town came into view.

"That's Avalon!" I said, practically choking on a potato
chip.

Helen looked up as I nodded toward the display.
"Huh . . . sure is," she said, unimpressed.

"Ever been?" I asked.

"A few times growing up, but I haven't been there in
years. You?"

"Several times," I said. "Went last spring with a friend.
We tried to mountain bike there. Wanted to explore the
fire roads and the rest of the island but found out you can't
go beyond the fences on the outskirts of Avalon without a
Catalina Conservancy Pass, which was like thirty-five dollars each. We spent that money at a bar overlooking the
beach, so we didn't get into the interior."

Helen ate for a minute, then looked up at me. "You just gave me an idea," she said and pulled out her phone and turned it on. "I have pics of the files in here somewhere..." She scrolled through her photos, concentrating.

"What's your idea?" I asked.

"Ah! Found it!" She had her index finger on her phone screen and looked up at me. "When you mentioned the Catalina Conservancy, it reminded me about Debbie—she's the woman with the three arms..."

"Oh, I won't forget her. Don't worry," I interjected, smiling.

"*Any*way, remember that she was on the city council that denied Basking Enterprises the land they wanted to build on?"

"Yeah," I said.

"It's all in her files—something I'll bet neither brother has ever looked into, but I did as part of my research on all the experiments." She scrolled through more photos. "Oh, here it is. Debbie's uncle is a voting member of the California Coastal Commission, but before that job, he was a deputy director of the National Park Service."

"Still not sure where this is going," I said.

"Maybe Debbie's uncle can hook us up with some land on one of the Channel Islands. A sanctuary, remote and secluded, where they can live in peace as they reacclimate."

CHAPTER FIFTEEN

Unbearable. This new word bubbled into Albert's awareness as he was jostled about in the back seat of his car. The pain *seemed* unbearable, yet he was obviously bearing it, so at what point does bearable become unbearable? Fixating on this seemed to ease his suffering just a bit, but as he considered it further, a sharp zap shot through him as if his spinal cord was welded to an electrical panel. He passed out again. He awoke a few moments later. These short-term losses of consciousness were happening more frequently, and he realized this torturous cycle marked the boundary—the knife's edge between bearable and unbearable pain. Bearable - conscious, unbearable - *snap* - unconscious, and so it went, mile after mile, a relentless pendulum. During a moment of awareness, he felt the car go over large bumps. *Speed bumps*, he realized. *A parking lot.*

The car came to a stop, and he felt the vehicle shift as Arlene exited. She closed her door, and he heard the soft click of the rear handle.

"Ready for this, Doctor?" she said, reaching into the back seat. She had to pivot her shoulders to flop the dead head out of the way, then lean at an awkward angle to keep it from swinging in front of her field of vision. "Jesus, Doc, don't take this the wrong way, but you stink." She reached in and grappled with the black curtain he was wrapped in, trying to get her arms under the gelatinous mass that was his body.

"Eerrooughlel!" Albert howled, sounding more animal than human.

"I got ya, Doc," Arlene said as she struggled to kick the car door closed while holding him. She heard something crack from within the shroud, and Albert let out another yelp. She looked down to see all manner of bodily fluids leaking from his shroud, spattering on the pavement. "How are you even still alive?"

"Uhnberrribble . . ." he eked out, more slobbering gibberish than a spoken word. Then, snap!—the world went dark again.

CHAPTER SIXTEEN

B y the time Helen and I finished dinner and talked for an hour or so, we were both exhausted. This whole time, Grinder sat quietly, reading, having borrowed a book from Otzi. If the sight of a bathing-suit-wearing half-man, half-gorilla sitting in a chair reading a book still seems odd to you, then you haven't yet grasped the surreal reality that has become my new existence. I had so many moments that day where the lines between the fantastical and the ordinary blurred that it seemed to be boosting my capacity to adapt and empathize. I was, somehow, tuning into the frequency of this new world, where every anomaly I witnessed wasn't a cause for alarm but a reminder of my ever-expanding horizon of normalcy. The question "What is normal?" finally had an answer: "Nothing."

"You'll want these," Grinder said, sliding two air

mattresses through the bars. "They're self-inflating. Just turn the valve there at the end."

"Thanks, Grinder," Helen said as he walked back to his chair. He said nothing, just waved his arm up in acknowledgment.

Sleep came quickly, but I was restless, tossing and turning throughout the night. Helen didn't seem to move at all. When I finally decided I was done trying to chase sleep any more, I looked at my phone and saw that it was just before 7:00 a.m. I lay there thinking, waiting for Helen to wake up. I figured at least one of us should be well-rested as we greeted whatever the day had in store. I wasn't worried so much about Bernard offing us; he didn't seem like the type. His brother? That was another matter. Luckily, we left him to baste in his own juices. Literally. Helen stirred a little and gave a "mumph" as she turned toward me, her eyes fluttering open.

"You snore," she said, squinting against the fluorescent lights overhead.

"You sleep like you're dead. I wonder what they serve for breakfast around here?"

I sat up and saw Grinder sleeping on a mat next to his chair. Otzi was somewhere, likely on his bunk, which was in the shadows.

"We're going to have to get somewhere that our phones work," I said.

Helen brushed the hair from her face, yawned, and sat up next to me. "Yeah, there's got to be other paths to the surface."

At that moment, there was a clatter as the door swung open and Zach, Bodie, and Dax walked in carrying food trays.

"Wake up, slacker. Chow time," Zach said to Grinder, who stirred and climbed onto his chair. Zach handed him a tray but tipped it a bit and the bowl slid onto Grinder's lap, spilling hot oatmeal onto his shorts.

"Shit!" Grinder said, jumping to his feet. "You did that on purpose!"

Bodie and Dax chuckled as they approached our cage, sliding our trays through the small slot at the bottom of the door.

Zach got into Grinder's space and stood looking down at him. He was still an adolescent but was heading toward being a silverback, a troop leader. Zach towered over Grinder, taking an intimidating stance. Even from where I was, I could see his fangs showing as he talked.

"Listen, little shit," Zach said, low and mean. "Anytime you want to challenge me, I'm here for it. You're a class-A weasel, and there's no place for you in our troop!"

I turned to Helen's ear. "That's the gorilla in him talking right now. This is a classic fight for dominance."

"Let me guess—you learned this last semester in your anthropology class."

"I did!"

"You sure it isn't *human* bullying?" Helen asked.

"Okay, a combination of both."

Our attention was drawn back to Grinder and Zach as Grinder threw his food tray to the ground and cleared his space by kicking his folding chair backward. The chair smashed into Otzi's cage. He then got as close to eye to eye as he could with Zach, who stood several inches taller than him.

"I'm so sick of your bullshit!" Grinder spat. "If this is what you want, then fine—let's do this right now!"

Zach moved forward, closing the small gap between them. Bodie and Dax rushed over, and each of them grabbed Zach by a formidable bicep. "Easy there, big guy," Dax said. "This isn't the time or the place."

Zach shook the two loose and turned, baring his teeth at them. He turned back to Grinder. "I'm waiting," he said, grinning.

Without hesitation, Grinder unleashed a devastating right uppercut to Zach's jaw. Zach staggered back, tearing himself free from Bodie and Dax. Grinder didn't wait for Zach to recover. He leaped forward, placing himself in front of Zach and throwing a swift left hook into Zach's ribs. Zach doubled over, now forced to recover from two more blows. Grinder was on him, beating on his back like a drum, delivering blow after blow. Bodie rushed in and tried to grab Grinder, but Grinder spun back, planting a well-placed fist into Bodie's midsection. By the time he pivoted back, Zach was rushing right at him, head down. Zach lurched up and grabbed Grinder by the forearms, shoving him back, trying to knock the smaller gorilla off balance. Bodie and Dax followed the brawl as it moved past our cage and toward Boris's. Grinder managed to wrench one of his wrists free from Zach's grip and spun his body, coming up behind Zach in a move that could only be described as balletic.

Grinder used his leverage to bring Zach's hand back behind him, putting Zach in a headlock with his own arm. Zach released his grip to get better leverage and Grinder used that moment, delivering a kick that sent him headfirst into Boris's cage. *CLANG!* Zach hit his head hard. Boris stood just inches from Zach, nostrils flaring, prominent fangs showing beneath curled lips. The air between them thickened. Boris's gaze, intense and unwavering, held a depth of authority and wisdom. His eyes communicated a clear and powerful message with no need for words.

The fight was over, leaving Zach and Boris in a bubble

of silent confrontation. Bodie and Dax stood their ground, watching. Otzi came forward to his bars.

It seemed Boris's stare was not just a display of dominance; it was a declaration of protection over Grinder and a stern warning, conveying a blend of strength and leadership and an unbreakable resolve that seemed to resonate with Zach on an instinctual level.

Zach, despite his own formidable presence, found himself submitting to the silent command emanating from Boris. The giant silverback's posture, unyielding and majestic, combined with his steady and commanding gaze, spoke volumes. It said that he was the true leader, the alpha of their troop, and his protection extended to all members. The message was clear: any disruption of the peace within their group would not be tolerated.

Zach slowly straightened and took a step back. Grinder, witnessing this exchange, took a deep breath and looked on. The silverback's intervention took place without violence, from within the confines of his iron cage. It seemed to have reaffirmed his leadership and the unspoken rules that governed the troop's interactions. As the dust settled and the fighters moved to their own spaces, the hierarchy within the troop was once again solidified.

Zach glanced up at Grinder as he passed him. "Stay here until we figure out how to get rid of these two."

Grinder gave the slightest of nods, then turned and

gathered the items onto his tray. As the other gorillas exited the room, he sat but ignored his food, alternating between staring off into space and peering toward Boris's cage.

"You guys shouldn't have come here," he said, picking at his food and shaking his head. "Bernard doesn't need an excuse to incinerate things he has no use for. He enjoys watching things burn."

I spoke up. "So, Bernard makes an extreme effort to save people like Scott but just flicks a switch and eliminates anyone who doesn't meet his needs? Seems he's got a God complex like his brother."

Grinder stayed silent. Helen approached the bars. "Grinder? Do you want to get out of here?"

I walked up to the bars near Helen, but she waved me back. "I got this," she said.

That made sense, I thought. Take it slow and easy—one on one. I went back and sat on the air mattress.

Helen spoke gently to Grinder, who continued to look down at his tray. "We're working on a plan to get us all out of here, but we can't do it without your help." She waited a few moments, but Grinder didn't look up, so she turned to walk back to me.

"I won't have any say on what happens to you guys," Grinder said. He set his tray on the concrete floor but didn't look up. "I'm glad Boris did what he did there, but he shouldn't have had to. Zach and I used to be good friends. We went through high school together. He surfed, I skateboarded. We had the same friend group."

Helen turned back to the bars but didn't walk toward them. "What do you think happened, Grinder?"

"That's a combination of your gorilla DNA and living in confinement," Otzi interrupted. Boris gave a low chuff behind us. "Your *aggressive* tendencies are running un-checked, and you have near zero impulse control."

"That's exactly how I feel—all the time!" Grinder said.

"And it will probably get worse," Otzi said, now stand-ing at the bars of his cage. "I've been around a long time." He chuckled at the understatement. "And I think you just can't keep certain species captive. Goats, cows, chickens, sure, but gorillas? No way. Eventually, even in the best zoos, gorilla troops need to be managed, their occupants evaluated, moved around to other zoos, sometimes iso-lated—it's just something that happens. You may not be in a cage, Grinder, but you are still a captive and you'll be-have that way."

"Humans?" Grinder asked, looking at Otzi. "Can you keep humans captive?"

Otzi gave a short laugh. "Look at any prison system and you tell me."

I stood and walked over next to Helen. "Otzi, would you be interested in having your own hut on an island?

Your own garden?" Otzi just looked at me, expressionless. "A place you could fish every day?" Otzi grinned. "We still have a long way to go with this plan, but one thing's for sure: it won't happen as long as we're stuck in here."

We walked back and sat on the air mattresses with our backs to Grinder and Otzi. Boris was in front of us, his hands on his bars, watching and listening. I took another antibiotic and Helen redressed my leg.

"Let's remove this head bandage now," she said.

I let her skillful hands work on my wounds, and I looked up. Boris was still staring at us.

"Hi, Boris." I nodded a greeting toward the enormous silverback. He curled his lip up a bit, revealing a few of his teeth.

I turned toward Helen. "Suppose that's a smile?"

"You go right on believing that," Helen said. "It could be the last look he gave Scott."

"Good point."

We sat there for a few minutes. "His eyes are so expressive, so human-like," I said.

"I think you have it backwards," Helen said. "Our eyes are so expressive, so gorilla-like."

"Damn, you're right. For a second, I forgot we share a common ancestor."

There was a clatter behind us, and we turned to see Grinder fumbling with his set of keys. "I'm in, but we need to move fast . . ." Grinder said just a moment before the door to the prison room burst open and all the gorillas, led by Mohawk, stormed in. Bernard walked in swiftly behind them, his face a mask of rage. Grinder stealthily dropped the keys into the pocket of his shorts. Boris was going nuts in his cage, banging on the bars and tossing things about.

"Quiet that gorilla down or tranq him!" Bernard yelled.

I looked past the fracas between Grinder and Mohawk and saw that Otzi had both arms through his bars. He was gesturing toward Boris by patting the air from side to side with his palms facing down. I realized he was asking Boris to calm down with sign language. I turned back toward Boris, and sure enough, he was looking at Otzi and he got the message. He calmed down almost immediately. Glancing back toward Otzi, I saw him sign two more gestures. Then Boris returned some signs and walked back toward the cot in his cage.

Bernard walked over in front of us. "Nurse Helen Hives," he said. "For the last twelve hours or so, I was struggling with what to do with you, but it seems you've sealed your own fate. I'd like to thank you for unburdening me with that struggle."

He turned and waved his arm toward Zach, who opened the double doors to the room and stood to the side as Debbie, Peter, and Jaguarman were escorted in by the other gorillas. Customized cattle prods with glowing orange tips kept the three bound captives in line as the gorillas guided them toward their cages on the other side of the room. All the gorillas exited the room, leaving the doors open. Heavy grunts echoed in from the hallway, and we watched as a flatbed cart creaked into the room, its cargo—the massive fire-breathing bear—currently asleep. It took all seven gorillas to push him into his cage. They left him on his cart, snoring like distant thunder.

The gorillas walked back over behind Bernard, who looked back at us.

"In the theater of life, not all characters make it to the final act. Your curtain call, Nurse Hives, is long overdue," Bernard said, then turned toward the gorillas. "Put Helen and her friend in the cage with the bear. Milton, fall in line with your troop!"

As the gorillas approached, Helen spoke up. "Find Albert yet?"

Bernard's eyes burned into Helen's. "Why, what did you do?" he spat.

Before Helen could answer, Scott burst into the room, gasping for air, his octopus arm reaching out toward Bernard. "Doctor, come with me. It's about your brother."

CHAPTER SEVENTEEN

Grinder walked out of our cage, and the rest of the gorillas corralled Helen and me into the cramped cage with Smokey and locked the door. We turned to look at the sleeping behemoth. Even in his slumbering state, he looked every bit the nightmare creature we witnessed a few hours ago, except we were now close enough to smell the beast. As we stood there, our backs to the bars but still less than ten feet from Smokey's head, he shifted. His snoring stopped for a long moment, and he rolled to his other side, facing away from us. The cart beneath him creaked under his tremendous weight. Helen, Grinder, and I took furtive glances at each other, then back at Smokey, who hadn't resumed his snoring. From where we stood, we could just barely see over his massive torso to his head. We watched in silence as he moved again, this time bringing an arm up to scratch his nose.

"He's waking up!" I whispered to Helen, who simply stared straight ahead, frozen in fear.

I looked around for any way out of this. I could see Jaguarman, Debbie, and Peter all watching from their cages nearby.

Smokey took in several raspy breaths in quick succession and then reared his head off the flatbed and unleashed an ear-splitting sneeze. A burst of flame shot from his mouth and nostrils and dissipated just beyond the bars. As soon as he recovered, we scooted a few feet to our left to avoid being in the path of any further sneezes. A low rumble emanated from Smokey's throat. I could feel it beneath my feet and resonating in my chest. This wasn't a snore, I thought as I watched Smokey move his legs and head, obviously waking up.

"This is one helluva grumpy bear," I said to Helen quietly.

I turned toward the bars and tried to spot a weakness in the structure—nothing. Smokey grunted and groaned as he woke, moving from side to side, trying to shake off the effects of the tranquilizer. As he rolled again, I turned and caught a glimpse of one of his eyes, and I'm pretty certain he saw me as well, because the eye widened as it flashed by me. Smokey released another tremendous groan and then sat upright. He stared at us through bloodshot eyes.

"Hey, guys." There was a voice from close behind us, and we spun to look; all the while, Smokey was struggling to stand.

"What the hell?" Helen said to Otzi. He stood before us, wearing a welcome, slightly nervous smile, his bow and arrow trained on Smokey.

"Thought you guys could use some backup," Otzi said, his eyes still trained on the bear.

"We could use a key," I said.

"No key, but I might have something better," Otzi replied.

"Otzi, I hate to remind you, but that arrow has a suction cup on the end of it," I said.

Otzi just smiled and kept the arrow aimed at Smokey. He nodded at the bow. "Not this! This is just a prop. I'm hoping this bear is smart enough to see a threat but not smart enough to see it's fake."

"Helluva gamble!" Helen said.

"I know," Otzi said. "That's why I'm relying on this." He passed the bow and arrow through the bars to me and turned toward Boris's cage. I held the toy for a few seconds, contemplating its usefulness, then dropped it to the ground.

What happened next could, under any normal circumstances, be described as extraordinary, but today it was just one more jaw-dropping event. Otzi walked over to Boris's cage and stood a couple of feet from the huge ape.

He started signing—using ASL, from what I could observe—and the gorilla signed back, not in the slow and deliberate manner that we witnessed from the likes of Koko the gorilla back in the seventies but with the speed, skill, and dexterity of any ASL signer. Even Smokey seemed to forget we were standing there and was watching the exchange. At one point during their conversation, Boris seemed upset. He rattled his cage door, then walked deeper into his cage for a couple of seconds, then charged back toward Otzi, beating his chest. After a moment, they resumed their chat in a blur of gestures. Otzi remained calm, and after about a minute, he walked back over to us.

Smokey resumed trying to stand, and he shook his head again, obviously still dizzy.

"Okay, this should work," Otzi said, then turned back to Boris and signed something. We all watched as Boris stood, facing us, his hands on the bars, posture erect, muscles tensing. He grimaced as he pulled on the reinforced iron. "Boris doesn't know that he has the strength to bend his bars. It wasn't easy to convince him . . ." We heard a creaking sound and watched in amazement as the solid carbon steel bars began to bend. Smokey, now standing shakily, held on to the cage and watched as well. "I did the math on this over a year ago. He could bend bars twice that diameter if he tried. Being in captivity all his life, he never thought to have a go at it."

We continued to watch as Boris wrenched the bars to the point of breaking. There was a sharp *twang* as a broken crosspiece flew out and caromed off Debbie's cage. Otzi's words had barely faded when Smokey, now fully alert and with a newfound curiosity sparked by Boris's actions, edged closer, his immense frame blocking some of the overhead light and casting a long shadow over us. The air hung heavy with anticipation and the metallic tang of exertion. Smokey was no longer glaring at us like we were fixings for his next barbeque. He set his eyes on Boris, watching intensely, as if understanding the possibility of freedom for the first time.

After Boris escaped from his own cage, he went to release Jaguarman, Debbie, and Peter. For whatever reason, Smokey was now grooming himself in slow movements, seemingly happy as a clam. At one point, he moved his head in close, the pungent smell of burning hair assaulting our nostrils. Helen reached over and scratched behind his ear. He liked that so much that he moved in even closer, now pinning us against the bars. I scratched his head, too, and he let out a soft rumble that must have been his version of purring.

"Okay, big guy," I said, struggling to move away from his gargantuan head. He moved back and resumed grooming. "I guess we're okay as long as he doesn't sneeze again."

Helen nodded, then turned to Otzi. "How did you get out of your cage?"

Otzi smiled. "My door hasn't been locked for a couple of years. I pose no threat to anyone and can't make it on the outside, so Albert just unlocked it one night over a couple of brandies and never relocked it. This is probably the first time I've needed to be outside of it in a year."

Boris, Debbie, Jaguarman, and Peter walked over to our cage and wrenched the double gates open. We exited and Smokey clambered out.

"Thanks, Boris," Peter said, stretching his tail out.

"Hey, your tail regrew!" I said, pointing at its tip.

"Lizard DNA," Peter said, smiling.

"Now what?" Debbie asked.

Helen looked at Debbie, then scanned the rest of us. "Now we get Max, then head to the surface. By the way, does your uncle still work for the Coastal Commission?"

CHAPTER EIGHTEEN

A rlene's question—*How are you even still alive?*—echoed in Albert's mind and served as his latest distraction as she carried him to his new caregivers. He looked up at Arlene as she leaned over to place his limp body gently on the gurney. Her one head, the picture of strength and composure; the other head, gray and useless, a rotting reminder of one of his first major experiments. *She'll get the operation*, Albert thought. *I'll fix what is needed because I can. Because that's what a loving god would do.*

The bright fluorescents stung Albert's eyes, and he found that closing them didn't seem to help much. That was partly because his pupils were dilated from him being in shock and partly from his eyelids being reduced to thin, nearly translucent membranes. As the gurney began moving, he could hear voices, some muffled, some coming through clear as a bell.

"He's a bag of bones!" someone exclaimed.

"What's keeping him alive?" another person said, reinforcing Albert's conviction of immortality.

"Silence!" Bernard roared at the medical assistants as he joined the team wheeling Albert into the medical bay.

When the gurney finally came to a stop, an even brighter light shone on him. He could make out the vague outline of a tall, thin man stepping in close.

"Beeerrrnharrd," Albert choked, his voice barely a rasp.

"Quiet now," Bernard said and moved to place his hand on his brother's shoulder. He stopped as he realized there was no shoulder on which to place it. He took a step back to take in the sight before him. Here was a naked, nearly skinless approximation of a human form. Albert's body, if it could still be called that, was an eerie paradox—what should be dead wasn't. Where it existed, his skin clung to his frame like damp parchment, stretched so thinly over his bones that each rib and vertebra was pronounced. His limbs, devoid of their muscular definition, were skeletal appendages, more akin to the delicate limbs of a bird than those of a man. The contour of his skull was visible beneath the fragile canopy of his scalp, with patches of hair clinging desperately to the surface. His nose and lips were gone, leaving the nightmarish visage of a living skeleton.

Bernard was saddened by what he saw, but he was also intrigued. A thin smile grew across his broad lips. If he could keep his brother alive, he could create something magnificent.

PART FOUR

I miss my family. My wife. My children. The warmth of community. I know they are long gone, dust scattered across the ages. But the ache in my heart remains, a constant reminder of what I've lost. I long to share stories around a fire, to laugh and sing with those who understand me. Perhaps, someday, I'll find a place where I truly belong.

Otzi's journal – Ice Age Thoughts, April 2009

PART FOUR

CHAPTER NINETEEN

"Can we talk for just a second?" I asked Helen as we stood among the others, ready to make our break. Helen nodded, and we walked a few feet away. "I don't think it's realistic to think we can *sneak* a three-ton bear around an unfamiliar place. We might have to come back for Smokey."

She considered this for a few moments. "I hear you, but we can't get out of here, then come *back* for Smokey. Plus, think how effective he'll be at clearing the path if we need to."

"Okay, we can give it a try," I said and turned toward the rest. "We're going to start by going into the room behind Boris's cage. That, at least, will keep us out of the main hallway for a bit. Our first goal is to find Max; then we'll head for the surface." I watched as Otzi signed the instructions to Boris, but had a feeling Boris understood me anyway.

"Debbie, stay with me," Helen said. "The rest of you, let's go. Boris, lead the way. Someone make sure Smokey knows to follow us."

"I'll bring up the rear behind Smokey," Otzi said. "That way, if he sneezes, I won't get fried." He chuckled to himself.

I looked around, taking in the prison room, and noted the only cage that wasn't in total shambles was Otzi's. His display was still on, this time showing another sweeping aerial shot of a snow-capped mountain range. I remembered Otzi's bow and arrow and stepped over to retrieve them from Smokey's cage as we passed it. I handed them back to Otzi. "Here ya go, buddy."

He took the items happily and smiled, running his thumb over the arrow's rubber tip. "Thanks!" he said, following in line behind Smokey.

When we reached the feeding door in Boris's cage, he grabbed hold of the edge and wrenched the whole thing off its hinges in one pull, then turned and placed the door gently on the ground. Then he turned to us, a huge grin on his face, obviously proud of his newly realized abilities.

We walked through the narrow passageway, Smokey scraping the metal sides as he pushed through.

The meal prep room looked like any large industrial

kitchen. Stainless steel counters, cabinets, and refrigerators. There was a large island with a sink dominating the room.

"Hold up, everyone," I said, looking around. "Find something to eat here, and if you have any way of carrying food—for yourself or others—please do so."

The group started foraging, turning the otherwise spotless kitchen into a cluttered mess. We all ate as much as we could, choosing from a variety of fruits and vegetables. There were several containers of live crickets, which represented the only lean protein in the kitchen. These must have been a special treat for Boris, who dug into a bin and scooped up several handfuls, gobbling down the insects with delight. I noticed a backpack hanging on a rack and grabbed it. It was large enough to hold a few pounds of fruit and several bottles of water. We walked out of the room, our bellies full and ready for whatever lay beyond.

We entered a long corridor. It was brightly lit where we stood, but about one hundred yards in the distance, it crept into darkness. I gently elbow-bumped Helen. "There are cameras everywhere," I said.

"I see them," she replied, glancing up at one of them as we passed.

We kept walking until we approached a door.

"Hold up, guys," Helen said. The group gathered around her as she spoke. "Since we don't know where

Max is, we'll need to check every room. It's important that we don't make too much n—"

BOOM! CRASH! We all turned to see Boris standing in the now-open doorway, a tremendous smile on his face.

Otzi looked up at Helen. "You have to give me some notice so I can sign to Boris!" he said, a frustrated tone in his voice. "His newfound strength and confidence have got him all giddy!"

We all peered inside the room, which was an electrical room of some kind, nothing worth exploring. "Okay," I said. "If that noise didn't call attention to us and the cameras aren't being monitored, that means one of two things. One, the security system here is horrible. Or two, they know exactly what we're doing and are leading us into a trap."

"Nice pep talk," Peter said.

"Let's move," Helen said and started walking, taking the lead.

We walked for nearly two hours, checking dozens of rooms along the way. The complex was massive, the size of an underground city.

We walked a little further, and I glanced back to see Jaguarman slowing. He was standing, nose in the air, obviously smelling something we didn't. I walked back to him, cautiously keeping my distance in case the salad bar he ate for lunch wasn't enough. "Hey, what do you smell?"

"Smoke," he said, in a deep voice that carried forth with a growl. "Like the world's worst barbeque."

"Like burning meat?"

"And hair," he said. "Like animals on fire!"

"You sure you're not just smelling the bear?"

"Of course I'm sure!" he said.

"Okay, okay," I said. "Take it easy, big fella. Let's keep walking and I'll tell Helen."

He chuffed and started walking again.

"Ya know, Jaguarman doesn't talk much and so far I'm not a fan of what he says in general," I said to Helen.

"Why, what's up?"

"He's smelling burning animals." At about that moment, I realized I could smell it, too.

Helen and I looked at each other. "Anyone else smell something burning?" she asked our group.

The consensus was unanimous. Smokey had taken the lead and moved ahead to the next door.

Debbie ran up behind him and wedged herself between the massive beast and the entrance. She looked over at us as we approached. "We don't want this guy toasting the first thing he sees if this door opens. Can I get a little help here?"

Jaguarman and Peter helped her by gently nudging Smokey back, talking calmly to him as he backed up a couple of steps. At that moment, the door opened and a young man in a lab coat stepped out. He froze, his eyes widening as he took in the sight before him. He clutched his tablet to his chest like a shield, then spun and tried to run back inside, but Debbie grabbed him.

He opened his mouth to yell, but Debbie whipped her third hand around and cupped it. She dragged him back into the hallway and turned him around to face Helen and me.

Helen reached over and grabbed his tablet, which he fought to hold on to. She turned her head toward Otzi and Boris. "Boris, you and Jaguarman go into the room and secure it. Call in Smokey if you need to, but only if it's absolutely necessary. We're not here to kill people, just find Max." She turned back to the lab assistant. "We're looking for a dog . . . a golden retriever puppy. You seen him?" Debbie released her hand from around his mouth, but he said nothing, a look of terror and confusion on his face. "Look"—she glanced down at his badge—"Brett, the three hands holding you are attached to one of the strongest, most ruthless people you'll ever meet. One word from me and she'll twist your head right off your shoulders."

Brett opened his mouth wide and looked at us.

"Where's his tongue?" I asked.

"There's not even a sign he ever had one," Helen said.

Sure enough, as I looked into his mouth, I saw teeth,

gums, a palate, but no tongue whatsoever. Brett was chin pointing at the tablet, pleading for us to release it to him. "Let's give him his tablet," I said. Helen agreed, and Debbie released his arms but hovered over his back.

"No funny business," Debbie said into Brett's ear.

He took the tablet and tapped the screen. The tablet spoke. "I'm an assistant in the crematory." There was a pause as he tapped more. "I don't see every creature that comes in here." He looked up at us.

"Okay, Brett," Helen said. "But you know your way around here, so you're coming with us."

Jaguarman stepped out of the room. "You're going to want to see this."

Helen and I followed Jaguarman into the room. Debbie was close behind, a hand gripping Brett's shoulder.

The pungent smell of burning meat and hair mixed with a stink of rot that was almost thick enough to see. The room opened into a broad hallway, where we passed several furnaces of various sizes. I could see Smokey's massive frame moving within the room ahead. Jaguarman turned to us. "This isn't pretty." He turned back, and we followed him. The space was nearly as large as the containment room in Albert's lair. It was filled with cages, perhaps hundreds of them, and liquid-filled pods as well. There were creatures large and small, many turning their attention to us.

I turned to Brett. "What is this room used for?"

Brett tapped the tablet. "Bernard and his brother are building an army, but some creatures don't make the cut. This is a holding area. We can process about a dozen per day."

"Process?" Helen asked.

"Incinerate," Brett's tablet said.

The word hit us like a physical blow. "We have to find Max," Helen said. "Brett, can you show us where the new arrivals are held?"

Brett nodded, and he and Debbie moved to the front. Smokey was visibly upset, as if he understood more about this room than any of us. He was pacing several rows ahead, grunting and chuffing. I tried to not look in each of the cages but saw the things we passed, and many were haunting visions of experiments gone wrong. I felt like I was trapped in a recurring nightmare. I was trying to forget the things I saw in the bowels of Perfect Skin, but here were more of these poor beings, most demonstrating the desperate lengths to which the Basking brothers would go to sustain life to the absolute limits of science. Each creature bore little resemblance to its original physical form, if it could be traced back at all.

There were more human experiments, most floating in pods because their bodies couldn't support their weight otherwise. Some were without limbs, some with too many or misshapen ones. There were many experiments with multiple heads, and one with no neck, but with his head embedded within his torso. His face protruded from beneath his rib cage, eyes blinking and mouth moving with silent pleas. Then there were the cages with chimeras—dozens of them. I saw an attempt at merging a lion and a zebra. Like some demented cartoon, the lion head chased its zebra tail in relentless circles—hunter and prey locked in a perpetual, futile battle. I imagined Albert and Bernard laughing endlessly as they watched this wretched spectacle. Hatred crackled within me, electric and sharp.

Among their other breakthroughs in unbelievable genetic manipulation and reanimation, the Basking brothers had discovered something that could save millions of humans each year. They somehow had figured out a way around transplant rejection, yet they kept it for themselves, churning out one monstrosity after another for their own amusement. Of the many troubling thoughts I was having as I walked along, one stood out: for most of these creatures, death couldn't come fast enough.

Preoccupied by emotion, I found myself lagging behind. I started walking to catch up when I noticed a cage several rows over that contained a creature of tremendous size. As I got closer, I could see that it was Tembo, the gargantuan elephant from the containment room. He trumpeted upon seeing me, which sent vibrations drumming through my torso. For an elephant of so little brain, he certainly had the memory that his species is known for. He stuck his trunk through the bars, and I approached, reaching my hand out to meet it. We touched, which sent a chill down my spine. Such a huge yet graceful creature being kept in here was beyond cruel; it was barbaric.

"We'll get you out of here somehow," I said. Our eyes met, and we held our gaze, finally only breaking it as Helen called out.

"Joe, we could use you here!" she said.

I walked over to where Helen and the group were.

"Tembo is over there," I said.

"Couldn't miss him," Helen said. "Michael and Eddie are here, too." She pointed at two nearby cages.

"Whoa!" I said. "Is it my imagination, or has Eddie grown since we saw him yesterday?"

"I don't think you're imagining it."

Eddie the iguana looked to be well over twelve feet long. He was up on his hind legs and leaning against his cage. He flicked his forked tongue in my direction. Michael was in the cage next to him. He wasn't humping the enclosure this time, just sitting there, his spider legs bent at shallow angles, keeping his shell-covered body hovering a foot or so off the ground. The herd of tiny elephants was there, too, and ran up to the glass wall of their enclosure when they saw us.

When we reached Smokey, we could see what was upsetting him. Several bears in various forms filled three cages in front of us. One of the bears looked normal, but the other two experiments were anything but. Boris and Otzi walked slowly up to him and tried to calm him down. The rest of us arrived at a section marked *Quarantine: Recent Intakes*. My heart raced as we approached, and I hoped that, against all odds, we'd find Max among them.

Jaguarman, with his enhanced senses, was the first to react. He rushed to a cage at the far end of the room. "Max is here!"

We quickly assembled around Max's cage. He sprang to his feet, tail wagging happily. Helen's eyes welled, but her voice was steady. "We're getting you out of here, Max. And not just you—we're taking as many with us as we can."

Debbie spoke to Brett, her formidable presence looming over him. "How do we open the cages?"

Brett quickly tapped on his tablet. "If I help you with that, Bernard will take my eyes!"

Peter stepped in and unfurled his tail, wrapping it loosely around Brett's neck. "Without eyes, you could still breathe," Peter said and constricted his tail.

Brett, gasping for air, brought his free hand up and grabbed the muscular appendage around his neck.

"Enough," Helen said. "Brett, help us and you won't have to worry about Bernard's threats."

The tablet spoke. "These aren't just threats. Bernard removes eyes, ears, and tongues from anyone who breaks the rules. He calls it Wise Monkeying people."

"See no evil, hear no evil, speak no evil," Helen said. "I've changed my mind. Bernard is every bit as evil as his brother." She nodded at Peter, who released Brett but remained close.

Brett leaned over, rubbed his throat, and caught his breath. He stood, tapped on his screen, then handed the tablet to Helen. It displayed a digital layout of the room, with a central control system highlighted. "You'll need my access card, but many of these creatures can't walk or be moved. Many may not want to leave. They welcome an end to their misery."

"How do you know?" I asked.

"When you can't speak, you do a lot of listening," Brett tapped out.

Helen nodded. "We'll open the cages and those that want to join us can." She looked back at the group. "Boris, Otzi, Jaguarman, you're with Brett. Secure the control room and start the release. Debbie, Smokey, and I will start preparing an exit route. We can't afford any delays."

A plan was taking shape. The atmosphere was tense, charged with a mix of fear and determination. Our mission had expanded beyond saving Max; we were now embroiled in a rescue operation of unprecedented scale.

In the control room, Brett worked quickly, his fingers flying over the terminal as Jaguarman and the others stood guard. The first cages unlocked, sending a wave of confusion and panic through the imprisoned creatures. It was crucial to maintain calm, to prevent a chaotic stampede.

"The little elephants are going to get crushed," I said, turning to Helen and Peter.

"Will they all fit in your backpack?" Peter asked.

"It'll be cozy, but I guess it's as good a place as any. Give me a hand loading them."

Peter and Debbie gently placed the elephants into the pack, and I knew that I was now responsible for their safe passage to the surface.

Meanwhile, Smokey was getting more agitated. Peter was the first to notice the smoke coming from his nostrils. "He's gonna blow! I can smell burning hair. Someone needs to get that bear away from those cages!"

Otzi and Boris tried pushing Smokey along, but it was no use. The humongous bear refused to move. At one point, he glanced down at Boris and I could see his eyes were lava red with fury. Helen rushed past me, Max running alongside her. She and Max stood below the magnificent beast. There was a moment when I thought

Smokey was going to roast them both, but then something happened. As Helen moved back a few yards, Max and Smokey looked at each other. The huge bear exhaled smoke, and saliva the color of burning embers dripped from his mouth. Max's tail stopped wagging, and I noticed Smokey was calming down. From somewhere behind me, Tembo trumpeted, but Max and Smokey didn't break their gaze. Within a few seconds, Smokey had calmed and his breathing slowed. The cages surrounding him were now open and the bears that could walk were now out, surrounding Smokey. Led by Otzi and Boris, the group moved along toward the exit.

All the creatures that could move did, and we formed a parade of rescued and rescuers marching toward the corridor. We couldn't save everyone, not even close. So many of the Baskings' sick experiments were simply living tissue molded into grotesque creations too weak or malformed to stand on their own. Some resembled animals; others were barely recognizable as once-human. As I walked with the group, I noted the overwhelming stench of decay, a stark reminder of the cruel ambition that fueled the engine of this tortured zoo.

When everyone was in the hallway, we heard and felt Tembo bellow from just inside the door. He was too big to fit through, and it occurred to us that he must have been brought in through another entrance. Before I could even formulate a plan, Smokey and the other large grizzly trotted to the doorway and stood on their hind legs. They used their enormous claws, taking swipe after swipe at the doorway. Drywall debris and metal rained down on them as they customized the exit to fit their humongous friend. Finally, Tembo squeezed through and joined us in the hallway.

"If one of Bernard's goons didn't hear that . . ." Helen's voice trailed off as she took in the number now in our group. She could see the last of the creatures scampering through the door, climbing over the debris.

As I looked at this crew, my heart sank. How were we going to sneak a group of fifty or more creatures, including a thirty-thousand-pound elephant, up to the surface and make our way to freedom? The prospect seemed hopeless, even before we gathered these extra members of our group. I looked over and saw Eddie and Michael, who were sticking close together—the giant iguana seemed to grow before my eyes. Michael was smiling and climbing up the leg of a winged pig. "Michael!" I yelled. "Give it a break!"

He turned to me and slid back down the leg, looking embarrassed. *If pigs could fly*, I thought. The Basking brothers and their whimsical manipulation of the natural order reminded me of making creatures out of Play-Doh when I was a kid. *This is what happens when you think you're a god,* I reflected. *You play with life in all its forms, as if you own the lives you create, manipulate, and destroy. They are there for your amusement and serve no other purpose. Sickos.*

Brett's tablet spoke and refocused me. "There's a cargo elevator up ahead—maybe half a mile."

I looked over and saw Helen speaking with Debbie, so I jogged up to join them. "What's the plan?"

"As soon as we can get a cell signal, Debbie will call her uncle in San Francisco."

"It takes months or years to designate land for threatened species," Debbie said. "I don't know what he can do to help, but I'll send him some pics or maybe Facetime with him so he can see our situation."

"All we can do is put one foot in front of the other," I said, trying to calm myself with my own words. However, another idea quickly dismissed that thought. "Wait, what about Grinder?"

"Shit," Helen said. "Hey, Brett, if we wanted to find Grinder—err, Milton—where would he be?"

"Not anywhere near here. Opposite end of the complex," Brett tapped out.

"Well, there goes that," I said. "There's no going back at this point."

"I can call him," Brett tapped.

"You can? Do it!" I said.

Bret tapped on the screen. We could hear a phone ringing through the speaker, but there was no answer.

"Hang on," I said. "Can you call the surface from that thing? Is it cell-enabled?"

"No, it's locked into our firewall," Brett tapped.

—

As we continued up the corridor toward the elevator, we noticed a few of the doors were open. Smokey reared up and sniffed the air. Jaguarman ran up to him and signaled for the group to stop.

"There's a human up here—close," he said.

Helen and I rushed up and stood between Smokey and Jaguarman. "Who's there?" I shouted. "Show yourself."

There was a shuffling sound from an open doorway, and a young woman in tattered clothes darted across the hall in front of us to another open door on the opposite wall. Jaguarman started walking to that room, but Helen spoke up.

"Wait, I'll go." She walked slowly to the open door. The room behind it was dark. "We won't hurt you," she said, standing several feet from the doorway and cautiously leaning forward.

The girl moved from the shadows and stood just inside the doorway. She was young, maybe twenty, and her unkempt hair hung in ratty tangles over her shoulders. Her clothes were dirty and torn.

"What's your name?" Helen asked.

The girl moved into the doorway and glanced at our group.

"Cassy," she said, wiping her nose with her sleeve.

"Cassy, I'm Helen and this is Joe." She pointed at me.

"You're lost too," Cassy said.

"Well, we're trying to get out of here, but sure—at the moment, we don't know exactly where we are. What do you—"

"You won't find a way out," Cassy interrupted. "No one does."

I glanced nervously back at Peter, Jaguarman, and Debbie, who were all watching and listening.

"Is that what you're trying to do? Find a way out?" Helen asked.

Cassy looked at the ground. "I was. Now I'm just . . . surviving, like the others." She looked back up at us and swung her arm toward the hallway ahead. "The elevator won't get you anywhere."

"You said 'others,'" I said. "What others?"

She raised an eyebrow, and a slight grin appeared. "Other people, monsters, groups like yours. Did you think you were alone?"

I glanced over at Brett and motioned for him to join our little conversation. "I don't know what to think," I said. "Brett here was leading us to an exit . . ."

"No, he wasn't," Cassy said. "Don't you get it? This whole place is a prison! You leave one cage and think you're free, but then you realize this whole complex is one giant cage. You'll never get out of here."

Her words fell heavily on us. The taste of freedom quickly vanished as my mouth became dry and my head began to pound. Once again, mild shock descended. I grabbed a bottle of water from the side pocket of my backpack and heard the high-pitched trumpeting of an elephant as I did so. I turned to Helen and Brett. Jaguarman, Peter, and Debbie were with us up front, as well.

"We need to do a reset here," I said. "Brett, what the hell is going on?"

Brett tapped his tablet. "I haven't seen the surface in two years. I figured the cargo elevator would get us up and out, but wasn't sure."

"Shit," Peter said. "This all makes sense. We're all here for their amusement. The cameras aren't for security; they're for watching and recording how all this plays out. Scott and his sadistic friends are probably watching us right now, cracking some beers and laughing their asses off."

"This is bad, but we have to keep fighting," Jaguarman said. "Can't surrender!"

"I'm not sure I'm buying your theory, Peter," I said.

"Are you saying that all these cameras and motion detectors are just here as part of a closed-circuit reality show for the enjoyment of a few select idiots?"

Peter looked at Helen. "Look, Helen," he said. "You worked for Albert but had your freedom, even as you were undergoing his experiments. But the brothers didn't just recruit from within their employees; they kidnapped people who gave bad Yelp reviews, cut them off on the freeway—right, Jaguarman? Or just for fun! You do not know the lengths they'll go to amuse themselves."

"I wouldn't put anything past them," Helen said, looking at Peter. "How'd they snag you?"

"I had two Arby's franchises in Moreno Valley and was covering for an employee one night when Albert appeared in the drive-thru. He ordered a Jamocha Shake, but our shake machine was down. He was upset but polite. Didn't order anything else, just drove off. Turned out he was waiting in the parking lot for me to get off work. He must have come at me from behind with a chloroform rag because I don't remember anything after he got me. When I woke up in Albert's lab, I tried rolling over but couldn't. I looked down, and I had a tail."

Cassy spoke up. "You guys are the third or fourth group I've run into this month. One group was recaptured because they started vandalizing labs, but as far as I know, there are a bunch of other people wandering around down here. Don't forget, this corridor is at least two miles long with other hallways that branch off who knows how far."

"Have you ever gotten up to a level where you can see daylight? Were there windows?" I asked.

"The freight elevator goes up above ground, but the spaces up there are built like this one, except there are taller ceilings with barred windows along the top, way out of reach," Cassy said. "Oh, and there are ghosts up there."

We all looked at Cassy, then at each other.

"Three days ago, I would have responded with, 'There are no such things as ghosts,' but seeing what I've seen . . . Nah, I'm still calling bullshit," I said.

"That's fine," Cassy said. "Suit yourself."

Jaguarman moved to the front, leaning in close to Cassy. "Bring 'em on!" he growled.

"Let's get back to reality for a second," Helen said. "Tell me more about the top floor."

"I didn't even get off the elevator," Cassy said. "What I saw scared me so bad I rode the elevator back down."

"So, you're saying it's possible to escape, but you're too afraid?" I asked.

Cassy shook her head. "Every group that's come through here has done the same thing I did: taken the elevator up, seen what's up there, and come right back down again. From what they told me, the windows are out of reach. No doors to the outside, either. The ghosts are naked, violent, and fast. They swarm right at you as soon as they see you."

"I gotta see this," Helen said. "You red shirts want to join me?" She nodded toward me, Peter, and Debbie. We all nodded.

"Me too!" Jaguarman said.

"Oh yeah," I said.

CHAPTER TWENTY

C assy joined us as we continued toward the elevator. There were some open doors leading to dark rooms along the way. I thought I could hear things scurrying in the gloom, but we didn't stop to investigate. As with the Perfect Skin containment room, I was in awe of the grandeur of this place. It was obvious that the complex was overbuilt. The ambitious doctors had spent a huge amount of money creating this labyrinth of halls and rooms, perhaps thinking their operation would one day grow into them. As we continued walking, Cassy jogged up to us at the front.

"I know a shortcut," she said. "Make a right at the next junction."

Helen and I looked at her.

"No tricks?" Helen asked, raising an eyebrow.

"No tricks."

We turned the corner and were greeted with another expansive corridor that seemed to go on forever.

"You sure this is quicker?" I asked Cassy. She just nodded. "Brett, what do you think? Quicker this way?"

Brett shrugged, then drew my attention up ahead, pointing at the far end of the hallway.

I could barely make out some dark figures far ahead. It was hard to tell how far away they were, maybe a quarter mile or so.

"What is that?" I asked no one in particular.

"Another lost group?" Helen said.

I tapped Brett's shoulder. "Well? What are we looking at here?" He made no attempt to answer, just kept his gaze ahead.

"Look!" Helen said, pointing forward.

I looked and saw that the blurry dots had taken form. They were definitely humans or creatures, and they were heading our way as we walked toward them. I walked out in a wide arc, getting a good view of our group, doing a mental roll call.

"Joe, move back toward me and watch that other group up there," Helen said.

I returned to where Helen, Peter, and Debbie were and looked ahead, as instructed. As I moved, one dot moved in sync with me. I walked back out again, and whoever or whatever was ahead of us moved simultaneously in the exact manner.

"Is it a mirror?" I asked as I continued zigzagging. With each yard we advanced, the group became more defined, and we slowly realized that we must be walking into our own reflections.

I turned to Brett. Peter was behind him, sticking close. I was about to halt the group to figure out what we were looking at ahead when I saw Max tear past us and race up the hallway. At that exact moment, a small creature of some sort—Max's mirror image—raced toward us as well. We were now maybe two hundred feet from the mirror, and that's when I noticed something was off. The open hallway doors on the mirror side didn't match the open ones we were passing.

"Max!" Helen yelled as she started running after him.

"Wait, Helen!" I said, chasing after her. "This isn't a mirror!"

She slowed and turned. "What? What do you mean?"

By now we were a hundred feet away, and as we both slowed, we saw the two Maxs getting within just a few yards of each other.

"Max!" I yelled. He stopped and the other Max stopped, too. "Come here, boy!" Max stopped but didn't come back toward us. "This is not a reflection. Look at the open doors there and there."

"Wait, if this isn't a mirror, then what are we dealing with?" Helen's voice was edged with fear.

Just then, the space between us and the other group shimmered slightly, like heat waves on a summer road, distorting the figures briefly before settling back into clarity. It was as though reality itself wavered.

Max barked twice and ran back toward us. The other Max didn't move, breaking our synchronous movements. By now the rest of our group had caught up.

"Let's keep walking," I said. "Okay, this is beyond weird," I squinted to make out any distinguishing features of our counterparts. That's when it hit me—the not-Helen and not-me didn't mimic our movements exactly. They seemed to anticipate them, moving in unnatural staccato bursts. It was like they were watching and learning our movements rather than mirroring them.

Brett finally chimed in, furiously typing on his tablet. "It's the experiment the doctors were working on."

"Experiment? What experiment?" Peter demanded. "All they do is experiment!"

Before Brett could answer, a low mechanical hum filled the corridor, emanating from the direction of our doppelgangers. The figures stopped moving, their outlines blurring and then sharpening over and over, like looking through a camera while twisting the focus ring.

Suddenly, the not-Max barked, a sound so unnervingly

similar to Max's own bark yet carrying a metallic echo that sent shivers down my spine. Our Max responded in kind, his stance defensive, ears pinned back.

"This isn't just about reflections or mimicry. It's something far more advanced," Helen murmured, her gaze locked on the other group. "They're learning from us, trying to become us."

Brett tapped on his tablet. "The brothers couldn't create creatures fast enough to build an army; too many of them were too malformed to be of use, so they talked about building what they call a dimensional replicator. I had no idea it was a real thing. I thought it was theoretical."

"Seems like a lot of information to share with a crematory tech they didn't respect enough to let keep his tongue," Peter said.

"It was all in the files," Brett tapped out. He pointed to his tablet, then flicked open a folder icon. "All in here. They forgot my tablet had access to this information or didn't realize it did at all in the first place."

After glancing at the tablet, I looked back at the group in front of us. There were two large, shapeless masses that were sharpening and blurring, the mechanical hum still resonating around us. After a few cycles of focusing, I could see they were replicas of Tembo and Smokey forming in the back of their group. I refocused on the group's leaders.

"Look at their faces," I said. "Their features aren't defined. They look like . . ."

"Mannequins," Helen finished my thought. Then, without warning, the figures began to approach, moving with a deliberate, unnerving gait. Their features became sharper, revealing expressions that mirrored our own but lacked the warmth, the soul behind them. It was as if we were staring at shells, husks donned in our likenesses.

"Back up, slowly," I instructed, keeping my eyes fixed on the advancing group. "We need to regroup and figure this out."

As we retreated, the space we'd thought of as a corridor began to warp, the walls pulsing with a soft, bioluminescent glow. A fine mist began covering the floor. The open doors we'd passed earlier now shimmered with the same energy and reverberated with the pulses emanating from the nearby group.

"We're not just in Bernard's lair anymore," Peter said, his voice tinged with awe and fear. "This . . . this is something else."

I turned to where I thought Cassy was. "Terrific shortcut . . ." But I trailed off as she was no longer anywhere to be seen.

"Anyone see Cassy?" I asked. No one said anything. We kept walking backward until we reached a safe distance. We paused, the walls pulsating around us. The other group had stopped as well, their eyes—our eyes—watching us with an invasive intensity.

Helen spoke up, a sudden surge of confidence in her voice. "I know what this is. It's a convergence."

"And . . . what does that mean?" I asked.

Helen looked at me. "We're in what's called a zone of intensified potential." She looked at the other group for a second and gathered her thoughts. "Look, when layers between parallel realities or dimensions get too thin, the realities begin to overlap, intersect, or intertwine. This creates a nexus point—a blend of energies, matter, and consciousness from both worlds."

"Your 'New Word Every Day' calendar is paying off," I said.

"You're not the only one who learned things in college. Theoretical physics—junior year. Basically, the doctors have somehow devised a way to create this intensified potential. It replicates other creatures automatically, combining two dimensions into one, but it only works if the replication cycle can complete. Look . . ."

She pointed at the other group. They were milling about, more or less duplicating our movements, but not speaking. The other-Helen was pointing just like our Helen was.

"Now watch the other me over there," Helen said. She backed up out of my sightline and I focused my attention on other-Helen. I squinted to see better and realized her facial details faded as our Helen moved further back. I tried the same thing, keeping an eye on other-Joe as I walked backward. Sure enough, his features blurred as I moved away from him. His body outline became less defined, morphing into a rough, clay-like mold of a human form.

"They aren't fully formed yet," Helen said. "There's still time to destroy them. Anyone see *Invasion of the Body Snatchers*?"

"Yeah, the garden scene with the hoe," I said. "That one is burned into my mind."

Helen nodded. "We're going to have to destroy the replicants."

"But the closer we get, the more like us they become," I said. "What will happen if we actually get close enough to engage with them, to fight them?"

"We'll be at the nexus point," Helen said. "At that point, there will technically be two Joes and two Helens and two . . . of each of us. We can't let that happen. We need to destroy them from a distance."

At that moment, Otzi walked up to us. "Let's fry the motherfuckers."

"Otzi!" Debbie said, surprised. "You've been hanging out with Jaguarman too long."

Otzi looked back at the group and made eye contact with Jaguarman, who gently pushed Smokey to his feet.

The massive bear grunted, and he and Jaguarman walked toward us at the front.

"Debbie, put Max's leash on him and take him to the back of our group," I said as I handed her the leash hanging from my backpack. "We don't need two dogs with his power."

Smokey's double was now at the front of the other group. He stood with the same imposing posture but was cast in a soft glow, his deep-brown fur bristling as his hair stood on end.

I looked at Otzi and Helen. "How do we get him to, ya know, blow his top?" We all looked at Smokey, who seemed more interested than threatened by his twin across the way.

Just then, we heard a laugh and turned to see Cassy standing in one of the open doorways behind us.

"What the hell?" Helen said, but immediately there was another laugh, more of a cackle, coming from another doorway a little further back. It was another Cassy. Then a door opened next to our group, right next to Otzi, who turned just in time to meet the full impact of a roundhouse kick from a third Cassy. Otzi spun and hit the ground hard. Helen ran over and kneeled next to him.

"You bitch!" Helen said, looking up at that Cassy.

"Eat me, Helen. You guys are done," she spat.

Debbie dropped Max's leash and sprinted toward us,

meeting Peter as he unfurled his tail. The two of them ran up to that Cassy, with Peter using his tail to knock her off balance and Debbie finishing her with a side kick that sent her flying back through the doorway. At that moment, three more Cassys appeared, all with menacing grins, and surrounded our group.

"Told ya there were a lot more people looking to get out," one of the Cassys said, grinning.

I heard glass breaking and looked on the other side of Tembo to see a Cassy pull a fire ax out of its wall compartment. I glanced ahead of us and saw that our twins were all standing, watching, no longer mimicking our movements.

"What do you want, Cassy?" I shouted.

"It's been great, but you all need to die now," she said. "Your replicants will all work for the doctors, so thanks for coming, but I'm afraid time's up."

"We can take them on!" Jaguarman said, practically salivating at the prospect of a battle.

"He's right," I said, looking around at the multiple Cassys. "There's only six of them."

The Cassy closest to me started giggling and then pointed behind her. There, in the distance, was a crowd of Cassy replicants, hundreds of them, all running toward us. Helen, who had been tending to Otzi, who was still grounded after the kick, stood and saw them approaching.

"Get Boris," Otzi said, sitting up and rubbing his jaw. "He'll know what to do."

Without hesitation, Helen ran back toward Boris, who was standing next to Tembo, watching all the Cassys run toward us. She pulled on Boris's arm and guided him to the front. I was expecting Otzi to have to sign something to him, but there was only eye contact and a nod between the two, which seemed to communicate what Boris must do.

Boris worked his way to the back of our group and faced the onslaught of Cassys heading our way. He took a deep breath. Then, standing on his hind legs, he began grunting loudly. The grunts weren't as threatening as they were penetrating; the sound waves, low and long, rolled down the hallway. Now only a few hundred yards away, the group of Cassys started faltering but seemed to regain their momentum after only moments. Boris then beat his chest and grunted some more. He alternated between the two for the better part of a minute.

"What's he doing?" Helen asked Otzi, who had gotten to his feet and was watching the spectacle unfold.

"He's calling for help," Otzi said. "Look!"

In the distance, some ways behind the charging Cassys, was another group. They were rushing at high speed, closing the distance between themselves and the Cassys. I looked at Boris, who had stopped vocalizing by this point but was still standing, watching. The group rushing in on the Cassys comprised larger creatures and I could make out an outline on one of them, a spiked shadow coming off the top of his head.

"That's Mohawk!" I shouted and turned toward Helen. I glanced at Otzi, who just smiled.

"It's all of them," Helen said. "And more!"

She was right. There were dozens of gorillas in pursuit now, and as the first one caught up with the last row of Cassys, we watched as he grabbed two around the waist and tossed them into one of the open hallway doors. The others followed suit, picking off Cassys by the dozens and slamming them into the rooms as they went. Boris charged forward, grabbing two Cassys and casting them into a room like rag dolls. We could hear the Cassys scream in protest and frustration as they were flung into the rooms. I looked over at Brett, who was busy punching buttons on his tablet. I saw he had a layout of the hallway and was locking each of the doors after the Cassy replicas were tossed in, turning each green-lit door outline to red with perfect timing.

About a dozen of the Cassys made their way to our group, including the one with the ax, who went straight for Tembo. The gentle giant saw her coming and swung his powerful trunk, clotheslining her mid-stride. She flipped, released the ax, and splayed out on the smooth linoleum, spinning for a bit before finally landing against the wall. Peter, Debbie, and Jaguarman dispatched her and the rest of them quickly into a nearby storage room. Brett locked the door, and we stood in the hallway, watching the gorillas walk toward us; the only sounds were the shuffling of feet and the hollow pounding of fists on dozens of doors.

I took a second to look at our replicas and noted they were still milling about, not coming any closer, seemingly stuck in limbo. We would have to deal with them in a moment, but first, we needed to greet our gorilla friends. Helen and I walked back, and Otzi, Boris, and the others joined in. Mohawk and the rest of his surfer buddies approached us. I was surprised and glad to see Grinder with them.

"Well," Helen said, smiling. "That was about the most awesome thing I've ever seen."

Boris chuffed, stood, and beat his chest. Some of the other gorillas returned the gesture.

"Where are you headed?" said Mohawk.

"Up," I said, pointing toward the ceiling. "Taking the elevator to the surface and getting out of here. Unless you guys know an easier way out."

"Basking has us on lockdown," Blaze said. "He operated on his brother and then went to the infirmary with him. He locked things down several hours ago and we haven't seen or heard from him since."

Helen and I looked at each other, then back at Blaze. "Wait," Helen said. "Are you talking about his brother, Albert?"

"Yeah," Mohawk said. "Caught a glimpse of him when he was brought in. He looked like someone dropped a plate of lasagna on the floor."

"Sonofabitch," Helen said. "Figures he would live through something as devastating as that. Should have just shot the motherfucker."

The gorillas had a mix of fear and admiration on their faces.

"You were responsible for that?" Mohawk said.

"Yeah, no sense keeping that under wraps. We're getting out of here and we'd like your group to join us. Or you can stay here and work for Bernard and Albert, too, if he makes it, and never see the light of day again. Thing is, we have a plan, of sorts, to get all of us to one of the Channel Islands, where we can be free. Think it over."

"Can we borrow your giant friend here for a brief conversation?" Mohawk said, pointing to Boris.

"Sure thing," Helen said. "Take your time. We have to fry some replicants, so we'll be a few minutes."

Helen, Debbie, Jaguarman, Peter, Otzi, and I walked back to the front where Smokey was now sitting, eyes closed and blissing out. He was getting a good back scratch from Eddie the iguana, who was now about the

same size as the massive carnivore. Two other bear creatures were sitting next to him, awaiting their turn.

"Okay, Eddie," Helen said. "I'm sure that feels wonderful, but we need Smokey spitting fire inside of two minutes so we can clear this hallway of those . . . whatever the
hell they are."

Eddie stopped and Smokey opened his eyes, letting
out a grunt.

"Okay, big guy," I said, walking around to Smokey's
side. "See that big blurry ball of fur up ahead? He wants to
come over here and take one of these female bears and—"

"What are you doing?" Debbie asked, walking over to
me. "He doesn't understand you."

"Oh. Well, how are we supposed to rile him up? He
needs to blast these replicants before they form into us." I
turned back to Helen. "Any ideas how . . ."

Before I could finish, Debbie grabbed my shirt and
twisted me back to the front. "Look! They're moving toward us again."

"Look alive, everyone!" Helen yelled to the group.
"We're about to have company."

I was so busy watching the imposing scene forming
in front of me I hadn't noticed Smokey standing until he
grunted. He reared up on his hind legs and growled, focusing his attention on the other Smokey, who was trying
to do the same. The growl that came from the other side

was an ear-splitting roar that was absolutely terrifying. I felt someone grab my collar from behind and stumbled backward. Debbie released me.

"Stay back here," she said.

Helen came up close next to me. "This could get interesting," she said, grabbing hold of my arm.

Smokey and his twin paced and growled. The rest of the replicants were mirroring us again, shuffling toward us with a zombie-like gait. The closer they got, the more they looked like us and walked like us. Their facial features became clearer, too.

"Anytime now, Smokey!" I shouted.

"Don't distract him!" Helen said just as Smokey's twin crouched on his four legs and started charging at us.

"Everyone back!" I yelled. I looked over and saw Jaguarman saying something to Smokey.

We retreated as fast as we could, but the replicant army seemed to gain on us.

CHAPTER TWENTY-ONE

"Time for action!" I heard Jaguarman say, and he turned, faced his oncoming twin, then took a few quick steps and feigned a leap, thrusting his arms up but never leaving the ground. The trick worked. His twin, mimicking him, did leap, and as he reached the apex of his jump, Smokey spewed a powerful stream of liquid fire. The flames hit the replicant square in the chest, and we watched as the creature screamed, then contorted and twisted in mid-air. As he fell, finally landing only a few feet from us, we witnessed the true horror of the doctors' experiment. In every way, the replicant became Jaguarman—down to the finest details of his fur patterns. We stood in awe, watching a fully formed and exact replica of our friend crying out in agony as flames consumed him. Smokey stepped in, brushing us to the side, and shot another stream of fire at the replicant's head, putting it out of its misery.

I tore my eyes away from the gruesome scene and watched the group of replicants slow, then stop. They were several yards from us but already formed near-identical reproductions of our entire group. I looked at the other-Joe and other-Helen, and they looked at us. I could see other-Smokey rearing up again and turning his massive head, trying to spit fire. Only sparks emerged, a crackling sound like a small firework echoing around us.

"Let's try something. C'mon," I said to the four of us at the front. Helen, Jaguarman, Debbie, and Peter nodded, and I led them, moving around the smoldering replicant carcass, and we walked toward the other group. Smokey trailed close behind. The replicants moved back as we approached, with looks of fear in their eyes.

"Let us pass and what you just witnessed won't happen again," I said. Smokey grunted and rose up on his hind legs, smoke streaming from his nostrils.

The replicants conferred with each other. It was so odd seeing other-Joe and other-Helen speaking to each other and gesturing in our exact manner. They looked back at us, and other-Joe spoke.

"No, we are here for a reason, so we'll take our chances," he said, his voice and intonations now exactly like mine.

I turned to Helen and quietly said, "I really expected this to work, didn't you?"

She nodded, keeping her eyes forward.

I looked over at Jaguarman and Smokey. "Do your worst, boys. Just don't fight your twins—no twin contact!"

The ensuing mayhem didn't last as long as I figured it would. I turned away when the fighting started—a decision born out of an abundance of confidence in Jaguarman and Smokey to do what was necessary and an overwhelming desire to shield my psyche from witnessing something similar to the flaming calamity we saw just a minute earlier. I should have plugged my ears as well, as some of what I heard will likely haunt me for years to come. Note to future me: if I ever find myself getting torn limb from limb, try to have some dignity and not scream "mommy" over and over. That was embarrassing as hell. As far as I'm concerned, other-Joe deserved whatever was happening to him. Thank goodness our group and the replicants weren't equally matched. Had the replicants made contact with their human twins, the fight would have been a bloodbath with many losses on our team. Our ability to defeat our equally strong adversary was due to the fact that they had not fully matured yet.

I did turn back at one point when I thought the battle had ended and saw Tembo and Brett rush past us to confront their twins head to head. We should have stopped that, but there was no stopping Tembo once he set his tiny mind to something. As far as Brett goes, I have no idea what motivated him to attack his twin, but he didn't hesitate to dive into the fray.

When the two Tembos hit, the cataclysmic clash of the two leviathans literally knocked us off our feet. Their convergence was more than just the result of the gigantic creatures colliding. It sent dimensional shock waves in all directions that seemed to disturb the very fabric of our realities. When we scrambled to our feet, we saw one elephant standing and the other on his side, not breathing.

Not far from Tembo, Brett and his twin grappled. Then one of them spun and swept the other's knee, forcing him to the ground. He fell hard, his head bouncing off the linoleum with a hollow thud. Dazed, he stayed on the ground, propping himself up on his elbows. Smokey and Jaguarman approached them.

"Which one of you is the real Brett?" Jaguarman asked.

"I am!" the standing Brett said, holding up his hand.

"Wrong answer," I said. "Brett would never say that because he can't talk!"

Jaguarman pointed at the one who spoke and turned to Smokey and nodded.

Smokey took a deep breath and released a burning river of flames. Fully engulfed, the other-Brett took two steps, then teetered and fell.

Helen and I watched as Jaguarman and Smokey returned to our group, their blood-soaked claws still dripping, smoke trailing from Smokey's nostrils.

"Where's your tablet?" Helen asked Brett, who pointed with his chin to some place behind her.

"Let's get to the elevator," I said. "Everyone up—time to move forward. Keep your eyes straight ahead. Do *not* look at the mess in front as we pass. Trust me."

CHAPTER TWENTY-TWO

The freight elevator door was the size of an RV, which was a good thing. I took another head count, and with the addition of the gorillas, there were now sixty-three of us. When the door rolled up, Jaguarman stepped in front and held out his arm, stopping anyone else from boarding.

"For whatever reason," he said, "I believe that I've got more aggression and less fear than anyone here. I'll go and—" Boris, who beat his chest and chuffed loudly, interrupted him. Jaguarman waited until he shouldered his way up to the front. "I take that back. Boris and I will head up and scope things out together. We'll be back with a report of the ghost situation upstairs."

No one argued with him, so the two stepped inside, pressed a button, and were on their way.

Helen gave an overview of the endgame to the rest of

the group. When she was done, she and Debbie walked over to me and we sat, taking advantage of the few minutes we had for a much-needed rest. I carefully set my backpack on the ground and lifted the little elephants out, placing them next to us. I poured some water into a bottle cap and placed it on the floor for them. They drank happily, and I continued to refill the cap. I shared my remaining protein bars with the group.

"The biggest obstacles seem to be logistical," Helen said. "Like how to move sixty-plus creatures without ending up on the six o'clock news."

"We'll need a few semitrucks," Debbie said. "And a flatbed for Tembo."

"What about the sanctuary? Is that something that can actually happen?" I asked.

Debbie took a long pull on the water bottle, then thought for a moment. "I'm fairly confident my uncle will work with us on this. He and I worked on the Tule Elk State Natural Preserve and the Antioch Dunes Wildlife Refuge. He loves these kinds of projects. Plus," she said with a smile, "I'm his favorite niece."

"I thought you said most of those take years to push through and get funding," I said.

"Most, yes," Debbie said. "But with his connections in Washington and the high level of secrecy this is going to require, I think things will move pretty quickly.

Remember, we aren't just a bunch of mutants; we present a national security risk. If other nations captured us or got their hands on the doctors' notes or the photos on your phone, who knows how much damage they could do. No, our situation demands profound and urgent action. We might even get to meet the president!"

I thought about all the information on Helen's phone. That alone was enough to be a problem. I hadn't considered the prospect of enemy nations or other bad actors using the information we had at our disposal. Debbie and I talked for a minute but were interrupted by Helen.

"Hey, guys! I've got a cell signal!"

I gently returned the tiny elephants to my pack, zippering it mostly closed, leaving it open enough for them to breathe, and placed it on the ground for now. I looked at my phone. I had one bar of service, but Helen had two.

"The signals must be getting in through the elevator shaft. Debbie, let's call your uncle," Helen said, and the two of them walked to the other side of the elevator door to make the call.

Peter, Otzi, and Grinder walked up to me.

"What's the plan, boss?" Peter said.

"Plan is we kick some ass upstairs, then get the hell out of here," I said.

"What's waiting for us up there?" Grinder asked.

"That's right. You weren't here when the original Cassy told us about the ghosts up there," I said.

"Wait, what?" Grinder said. I took a few minutes to fill him and the other gorillas in on our situation.

Before long, the elevator dinged, and the door rolled up. Helen and Debbie joined us as we waited.

Boris was the first to emerge. He held his head low and walked on his knuckles over to his troop. Jaguarman came out, limping. He, too, looked disheveled.

"Well?" Helen said. "What happened? What did you see?"

"Just what Cassy said. Ghosts. Naked, violent, and fast."

"Okay. Were you able to kill them or . . . however you get rid of ghosts?"

"Can't kill what you can't catch," Jaguarman said. "Fast fuckers. Odd too. They were protecting something in the middle of the room. A large tank filled with red liquid. We only caught a glimpse of it before they swarmed us."

Boris slammed his fist on the ground. The troop reacted and Mohawk moved in, gently placing his hand on Boris's shoulder.

"Boris kinda freaked," Jaguarman said. "I can't blame him. At one point, there were ten or more of them climbing all over him. He couldn't get away fast enough."

"What happened to your leg?" I asked. "Did one of them attack you?"

Jaguarman looked down at his leg. "Oh . . . no, I, uh . . . I tripped over Boris as I was backing into the elevator. Kinda twisted it a little. It'll be okay."

"Can you go back up there with me and Joe??" Helen asked. "We need to see what we're up against."

"I'd feel better if Smokey came with us," Jaguarman said. "Let's leave Boris down here to calm down a bit."

The four of us gathered in the elevator, and Helen punched the button for the ground floor. I closed my eyes as the elevator started to ascend. Something told me I wasn't ready for what I was about to see.

CHAPTER TWENTY-THREE

Inside the elevator, I turned to Helen. "Any luck with Debbie's uncle?"

"She only had enough time to give him a quick overview, but she has my phone now and is likely talking to him more. He was very relieved to hear she was alive."

The elevator dinged, and the doors opened to a large room, just as Cassy had described. It was sparse. There were a few tables and a couple of shelf units against the far wall and a kitchen of sorts in one corner. Narrow windows close to the ceiling let in late afternoon light. Jaguarman punched the lock button on the control panel to keep the doors from shutting.

"What are we supposed to see?" I whispered.

"The room extends around to the right," Jaguarman said. "That's where most were gathered. If we walk quietly and peek around the corner instead of barreling in like I did before, we might get a view of what's going on."

"I'll take the lead," Helen said.

"You sure?" I asked but immediately regretted it.

"Why are you asking? Because I'm a woman? It's my mission and my responsibility."

I held my hands up and nodded.

We moved out of the elevator, Smokey taking up the rear. As we reached the corner, we could hear feet shuffling and the sound of voices. Helen gestured for us to stop. She walked another foot or so to the edge of the wall and peeked around it.

Her breath caught in her throat as she peered around the corner. The vast room stretched before her, not filled with the menacing shadows she expected but with figures moving languidly, many of them giving off a slight glow. These were the so-called ghosts, but as her eyes adjusted, Helen recognized them immediately. They were not ghosts but flesh and blood, moving with an eerie grace.

Helen stepped back and leaned against the wall, obviously shaken.

"What is it?" I asked, softly.

"The Eves," she said, tears forming in her eyes. "All of them."

With my hands on her shoulders, I gently moved around her to look. The room was lined with makeshift beds and scattered personal items, suggesting a dormitory of sorts. At the center, as if on display, was the pod, and I could see a figure inside it. A gorgeous woman, just like the Eve back in Albert's museum, but this one was encased in a liquid prison.

I ducked back and looked at Helen.

"We're getting them out of here," Helen declared, her resolve hardening.

She stood up straight and directed her gaze toward us. "Let me talk to them."

The implication was clear—*Don't follow me in.* We nodded, and she walked around the corner.

I moved forward, carefully peering around the edge as she approached the ladies.

"Sisters. My name is Helen," she said as the Eves turned toward her. "I'm Eve 19."

There was a moment of confusion as the Eves saw her, then looked back at the center pod. Helen continued toward them, slowly, and the women greeted her and cautiously gathered around her. After a few seconds, I couldn't see Helen over the heads of the other women, but I knew she was safe. Certainly safer than she'd been in a long time.

—

When Helen came back around the corner, she wasn't alone.

"Joe, Jaguarman, Smokey, this is Melanie, Rebecca, and Tanya, more commonly known as Eves around here, but not anymore. The rest of the ladies are working with Juliana, or Eve number one. She needs to learn how to breathe outside of her pod, so it will take a little while."

"Nice to meet all of you," I said. I looked over at Jaguarman, who still looked a little weary. "It takes a lot to scare this big guy. And the gorilla . . . heh, he's still recovering."

"Just doing what we had to do," Melanie said with a slight smile.

The ladies moved with a kind of somber grace, their forms silhouetted by the dim light emanating from within them. Without the soup to fuel their perfect skin, their true selves shone through. Lines of sorrow and joy traced a map of time and lived experiences. As with Helen, fine lines webbed the corners of their eyes. Their hands bore the subtle calluses of labor and the fight for survival. No longer the unblemished ideal once worshiped, they now held a deeper allure. It was the beauty of resilience, of survival.

It was their glow that lent them an otherworldly aspect, making it easy to understand how tales of ghosts had begun. Their movements, fluid yet weary, made them seem like specters, dancing in the faint light, a hauntingly beautiful reminder of what they had been and what they had become. Each Eve, a unique embodiment of endurance, their imperfections not diminishing their essence but enriching it, painting each with the brush of humanity.

As Helen spoke, her voice seemed to weave through them, a thread pulling them closer together. The ladies listened, their expressions a mixture of caution and curiosity, the flicker of hope rekindling in their eyes. As we moved into the main area, they all gathered around Helen, a congregation of spirits momentarily bound by a glimmer of newfound hope.

In the background, the soft glow emanating from the pod cast long shadows, adding to the ethereal atmosphere. It was a stark reminder of their past, and yet, in this moment of unity, it also illuminated a path forward. A path not back to the impossible ideal of perfection from which they were created, but toward a future where their worth wasn't measured by the flawlessness of their skin but by the strength of their spirit.

As I observed from the shadows, it became clear that these women were far more than the sum of their genetic makeup. They were survivors, each with their own story, their own scars, and their own dreams. And in their resilience, they were beautiful.

—

It took some effort to get Tembo into the elevator. The enormous elephant had to duck to get in, then pivot and sit so his head would clear. He did all this under protest. Finally, it took Otzi, who seemed to have a way with all creatures, to guide him into position.

"It's okay, big guy. We can do this. Let's go see what's out there."

Tembo seemed to listen to the old man and they stayed close to each other.

Helen was still with the ladies when Debbie showed up, excited from her conversation with her uncle James. Seems there's nothing like a potential national security threat to mobilize a ground plan of action. James was on board not only because he believed his niece; the photos she'd sent sealed the deal. His superiors wanted to get a handle on this situation immediately. The screenshots of the files and the photos from the lab and museum were only icing on the cake. Mobilization was quick and decisive. "Contain this *now*!" was the phrase most often repeated, according to Uncle James. I couldn't agree more.

Priority one was getting everyone safely out of the building. I would have felt better putting some miles between us and that prison. Helen seemed to think we were okay waiting in a nearby courtyard. Help would be arriving soon and there was nowhere else to go. I supposed she was right. We would only draw attention parading down Beach Boulevard with this crew. Attention that we didn't need.

Helen and I kept watch as the creatures emerged, stumbling around, getting their bearings. It was actually quite touching to witness their joy at feeling the cool breeze on their faces, seeing the wide-open sky above them. I leaned against a wall and closed my eyes for a moment, catching my breath. When I opened my eyes, I was taken aback yet again by the spectacle before me. Creatures that had never before seen the night sky were enjoying their freedom for the first time. Some rolled around in pleasure, while most huddled together, excited but apprehensive. We were safe for the moment, but who knew when another attack would arrive.

Helen reached for my hand, and as our fingers entwined, I felt a sense of ease wash over me. No matter what came next, I knew I could handle it, as long as we were together. I wasn't sure when I became so attached to her, but going through hell will shoot you from date number one to date number thirty in no time flat. We were a team; it was as simple as that. I didn't even have to wonder if she felt the same. The way she looked at me when our eyes met told me all I needed to know.

We watched the rest of the group slowly make their way through the oversized doorway and into the cool night. Smokey reared up on his hind legs, standing at least ten feet tall. I'd witnessed that a few times, usually preceding a fire storm escaping his mouth, but not this time. After lumbering out, Smokey stopped, sniffed the air, and stood, tilting his head back and staring at the sky. He stood there for a while, simply basking in the glow of the half-moon. I couldn't see his eyes from my angle, but I'd like to think they were open, taking in this new world not flooded by fluorescent lights. Jaguarman moved to his side, looking around, still vigilant, but with the ghost of a smile on his face, something I hadn't seen before that moment.

Otzi's reaction was, perhaps, the most profound of all. Once outside, he stayed close to the building, walking along the perimeter, glancing nervously about. After a few long seconds, he reached both hands out and let his legs follow, taking several steps from the courtyard into the parking lot. Swinging his arms around in circles and then twisting his body, he stretched every which way. He was thousands of miles and thousands of years from where his journey began, and I worried that it might all be too much for him. Then he turned and I saw his gigantic grin. Apparently, he approved of his new world, even if his current view was limited to the paved courtyard. It must be that great big sky overhead that thrilled him so, because he raised his hands in triumph, laughing at the moon.

Tembo, the largest in our group by far, lifted his trunk. I squeezed Helen's hand, afraid he'd let loose a trumpet that would surely draw attention, but he didn't. He simply sniffed the air, pivoting the tip of his trunk this way and that, getting a good whiff of his strange new surroundings. He made his way over to the only tree in the lot, lay down next to it, and went to sleep. The rest of us milled about quietly and kept a watchful eye, hoping for the promised help that was to arrive and praying that more trouble wouldn't find us first. Each car light that passed caused the group to freeze. There was no relaxing for most of us. We were still vulnerable and fully aware that any attention could thwart our plans. Why was Bernard allowing us to escape? Were we jumping out of the frying pan and into the fire? I asked Grinder and Zach as they approached.

"Why do you suppose Basking hasn't come after us?" I said.

"He has reasons for everything he does," said Zach, scratching at his arm. "He's a bastard but I think his sense of survival outweighs his vindictiveness, at least for the moment. He'll want to get to safety before he takes up the pursuit."

I looked down and noticed Max was resting quietly. I turned to Helen.

"You think Max had any part of Basking's decision to not pursue us?"

"Like how?" she said.

"Dunno. Maybe his powers of persuasion aren't limited to those directly around him."

She shook her head as she glanced down at him.

"Could be," she said, smiling. "Or maybe Basking just knows when to lay low. Most cowards do."

—

A low rumbling announced that someone was arriving. We tensed, wondering if it was friend or foe. A caravan of military semitrucks and a lowboy trailer, usually used for hauling heavy equipment, swarmed into the lot where we waited. They were followed immediately by dozens of other vehicles. The night came alive with well-trained soldiers and federal agents. An official from the Department of the Interior exited his black Suburban and stood staring at the scene, then zeroed in on me, Helen, and Debbie.

"Which one of you is Debbie?" he growled.

I stepped forward, with Debbie hanging on my arm. "She is. And who are you?"

"Sergeant Adams with the United States National Guard. We've been ordered to evacuate you all immediately." He glanced at Debbie, and I could read his mind as his eyes fell to her third arm. He hesitated for only a moment, his professional demeanor winning out even with this strange sight before him.

After verifying his credentials, we began to load everyone onto the transports. It went smoother than you might think. No one wanted to be left behind, but there was no pushing or shoving, either. The creatures worked together for the benefit of all and we were soon ready to go.

CHAPTER TWENTY-FOUR

I've never been in the armed services and had no idea how efficient a well-coordinated military effort could be, especially on such short notice. San Nicolas Island, the most remote Channel Island, was the chosen relocation site. The US Navy managed it, and they already had temporary housing there. Roughly two hundred military personnel lived on the island at any given time, and the Navy and other organizations already managed conservation programs there. They also used it for weapons testing, but we were assured that, aside from some nighttime booms that might wake us up, the testing area would be nowhere near our protective reserve.

There were many logistical dilemmas and even more ethical ones. The former Eves needed to be protected and slowly introduced back into society, but we didn't know how long their glowing skin would last. Helen seemed to be able to turn hers off and on at will, but that wasn't the case with most. It was interesting watching the military men and women interact with our group. Training had prepared them to handle a broad variety of situations, but none of them had experience with our crew. Still, their professionalism was admirable and comforting. Max was doing his part as well. He saw that some of the creatures, especially the bear-like ones, were very nervous, so he used his special powers to calm them as the soldiers worked.

Helen and I watched the group get loaded into the trucks.

"Better hand over your backpack with our little friends in it," Helen said. "Where is it?"

My mind flashed immediately to the first-floor corridor, the pack sitting somewhere near the elevator. Or did I give it to Jaguarman or Peter?

"Shit!" I said. "I left it downstairs! I've got to go back and get it."

I turned, ready to dash back inside, but Helen said, "Wait! Take a soldier with you!"

"You're right. Good idea." I jogged over to the nearest guy with a rifle and looked at his name tag. He was one of the older guys in the troop, maybe forty-five, built like a bulldozer. As much as I didn't want to go back, at least I'd feel better with this guy beside me.

"Excuse me, sir, would you mind accompanying me

inside to get my backpack? It contains some vital things that cannot be left behind."

"I'll get it, sir. You wait out here," he said.

"I'm not even sure where it is. It will be faster if we both go," I said. He hesitated for a moment, then nodded. We ran back into the building and around the corner to the elevator. I pushed the button. "Thank you, soldier, by the way—for all of this."

"No problem, sir," he said. "You can call me Carl. Gotta say, this is all a little bizarre."

"Tell me about it," I said as the elevator arrived. "Wait until you see what's inside my pack." We walked in, and the doors closed.

When the doors opened, I knew something was very wrong. The corridor was darker than before, and an odorless mist hung in the air. We stepped out, and Carl raised his weapon. I looked around near the elevator but couldn't see my backpack.

"It's around here somewhere," I said. "I thought I left it ri—" I was interrupted by the sound of voices that seemed to come from up ahead, but it didn't take long to find their source. As we stood looking down the hall, two shadows were moving through the mist.

"Sir, I'll need you to get back into the elevator!" Carl said quietly, raising his weapon. I heard the click of the safety being disengaged.

Knowing I couldn't leave the backpack down there, I also didn't feel this was the right time to argue. I backed up slowly and watched the forms in front of me take shape. The larger of the pair was a woman of formidable size, standing at least six and a half feet tall. She was cracking her knuckles as she approached, and I was pretty sure she was smiling. Her proportions were bizarre. She had one neck and one head offset between the broadest shoulders I'd ever seen on a human. There was a wound dressing on her shoulder next to her head. It was then that I realized this was the two-headed woman from the museum pods. Her dead head had been removed.

Next to her, another figure emerged, and although we had never met, I recognized his unique anatomy from Grinder's description. He had a muscular pink and purple tentacle draped around the woman's broad shoulders, the suction cups gripping her skin and drawing her close as they strode toward us. He was smiling, too. A disarmingly pleasant smile, showing far too many teeth.

"What about us?" Scott said, grinning. "Aren't ya gonna rescue Arlene and me?"

They stopped a few yards away.

"Welllll . . . ?" Arlene said. "Come on, sugar. Don't you want to party with us, too?"

Carl gripped his weapon tighter and pivoted his head to me. "Sir, are these part of your group or—" He was cut off by a tentacle slapping him hard on the side of his head. His gun discharged as he stumbled sideways, and the bullet hit Arlene square in the abdomen. She collapsed to her knees, Scott's tentacle helping to break her fall. Her eyes showed anguish and bewilderment. Scott kneeled next to her.

"Arlene!" he said, then turned to me, all attempts at friendly humor gone. Carl regained his footing and trained his weapon on Scott.

"What the fuck?" roared Scott. "What'd you do that for, you monster?"

As he jumped to his feet, he extended his tentacle toward Carl, grabbing the barrel of the rifle and flinging it away. It hit the ground and spun into the mist. Scott darted toward Carl, taking him down. Before I knew what had happened, Scott's tentacle was wrapped around Carl's neck and he was choking the life out of him. At that moment, I didn't know whether it made more sense to dive into the fray or search for the rifle. My answer came easily as I saw the soldier's buck knife on his hip belt. I darted toward him, hand out, ready to unsheathe the knife as the two fought. I was able to grab the knife, and as I jumped back to regain balance, I noticed Arlene starting to stand. She was holding her stomach where the bullet had entered, blood coursing through her fingers.

"You fuckers!" she yelled and charged. She hit me

mid-torso, tackling me to the ground. I held on to the knife, but she had my wrists pinned. She slammed my hand down hard enough to make me release the knife. Her strength was incredible. I twisted, but she held tight, her face a grimacing countenance of fury. I could move my good leg, so I kneed her in the crotch. She didn't seem fazed by that, so I did it again. I was pummeling her in a region that would elicit a reaction from any normal person. She moved her hands from my wrists to my neck in one quick motion and began choking me. I grabbed her forearms and twisted my head just enough to see Scott and Carl locked in battle.

Scott now had Carl on the ground, his tentacle still around his throat and his hand coming in hard on the side of his head. Carl was busy fighting his own battle. If I was to survive, I'd have to save myself. The knife was gone; my strength was no match against Arlene's fury. I was untrained, not especially fit, and already tired from everything the past day had brought. It was in that moment, as I was gasping for air, that I realized this was probably the way I'd die. I didn't have the strength to move, even against this person with a bullet in her stomach, her blood squirting out from the wound as she choked me. I was seeing stars on the periphery of my vision and could feel my world shutting down.

As my trachea began collapsing, some thoughts

came to me. I wished I had gone to the gym more, finished my martial arts classes, done a push-up or two. I had no plans on taking these regrets to the grave. This all just seemed so wrong. On the few occasions where I'd contemplated my final moments on Earth, I'd hoped they would be free from regret. I imagined myself dying peacefully and painlessly, surrounded by loved ones. As I locked eyes with Arlene, her sweat dripping onto my reddening face, her blood gushing onto my shirt, I realized there are some things in this world we simply cannot accept. I found a second-wind and flailed my body, attempting to buck Arlene off of me. It was no good. Though I was determined, she was simply stronger than me. Sometimes that's the way it goes. It's not fair, but nothing in life is fair.

CHAPTER TWENTY-FIVE

As my consciousness flickered and my vision narrowed, I saw a light, ethereal and warm, coming toward me. I'm not religious, so it took me a moment to recognize this as the tunnel of light experienced by those who'd reached death's door. It moved through the mist and coalesced as it approached. I wasn't sure how I was going to move toward the light with Arlene bearing down on my throat, but I figured there were greater forces at work here. I was right. Through blurry vision, I saw the light brighten as it approached. Then, suddenly, the pressure on my throat was gone. So was Arlene. The glowing entity lifted Arlene off me as easily as a blanket. It tossed her to the side, and she hit the hard floor with a loud grunt. I coughed and rolled to my side to see Scott release his tentacle from Carl and sling it around the being's neck. As my vision cleared, I could see her, the soft light emanating from her skin, the unmistakable beauty and mesmerizing presence of Eve 31 from the museum.

She unwrapped Scott's tentacle with the ease of someone removing a scarf. He winced in pain as she squeezed the appendage and drew him closer.

"You have a choice," Eve said. "Leave or die."

Scott's face was a mask of anguish. He twisted, trying to free himself, but Eve kept her grip firm.

"Fuck you, bitch!" Scott spat. They locked eyes and Scott's expression changed. Ensnarled by the power of her allure, he found himself, like everyone else who had gazed upon her, a prisoner of her radiance.

Still gripping his tentacle, Eve squeezed until her fingers dug into the flesh. Scott winced but didn't pull away. She squeezed harder. Even from my distance, I could hear the popping sound as her fingernails punctured the flesh and disappeared into pools of blue and yellow pus. Scott's grimace turned into a slight smile. Tears formed in his eyes, and he began weeping.

"I love you!" he said. "I want you!"

Their eyes still locked, Eve tore through the appendage, ripping it from him at the elbow and tossing it to the side. It hit the ground with a wet plop. Unaffected by the pain of the brutal dismemberment, Scott let his smile grow. His body surged closer to hers. Their faces were now an inch apart.

"More!" he commanded. "I want to be inside you!" He looked into her eyes with an intensity that bridged worlds.

"Certainly," Eve said with a smile.

He lurched forward and kissed her, and his hand moved to her naked breast, but as his lips and fingertips met the brilliant, translucent barriers, they didn't stop. They flowed into her as if slowly sinking into an ocean of light. She reached around him and hugged him intensely. His clothes shed to the floor as she absorbed his naked form.

When nothing remained of Scott, she stood still for a moment. The man inside her was dissolving into a featureless dark mass. Eve looked down at her own body and observed the cosmic light show within her. The bioluminescent particles sparked and swirled around the dark remnants of Scott as she digested him.

Carl and I stood in silence for several moments, unsure of what to say or do. Turns out, we didn't have time for either. The bullet hit Eve a split second before we heard the rifle discharge. Some twenty yards away, Arlene stood on shaky legs, still looking through the rifle sight. A moment later, she stooped, dropping the rifle down to use it as a cane, and nearly collapsed.

Eve stood with her hands over her midsection, one in front and one in back. Her face showed some surprise but no expression of pain. As we watched, an intense light glimmered and grew within her until we were forced to turn our heads. Even with my eyes shut, I could sense the hallway light up as bright as the sun. We heard a soft *tink*, and the light diminished. Turning back, we saw Eve picking the bullet from the floor in front of her and examining it. Arlene raised the rifle again, but Eve lifted her hand, palm up, toward her. The simple gesture was enough. Arlene slumped to the floor, the rifle clattering beside her.

"I think I've done enough for now," Eve said, looking at us. "This really drained me."

Carl and I walked slowly toward her. "Do you want to come with us? The trucks are loaded up and we have an island that will be safe," I said.

Eve smiled, and I tried to avert my eyes from hers for fear of becoming transfixed again. "That's alright, thanks," she said. "I'm going to rest a bit. Then I have a doctor's appointment I don't want to be late for." She smiled again and winked.

"What's your name?" I asked.

"Freyja," she said as she turned.

"Thanks, Freyja," Carl said, still enraptured. He apparently did not avert his eyes.

"You're welcome, gentlemen," Freyja said.

"C'mon, big guy," I said to Carl and grabbed his shoulder. I forcefully pivoted him away from Freyja as she strode back up the corridor. "We've got to find my pack and get topside."

My backpack was around the corner from the elevator. Perhaps someone in our group had stowed it there for safety. I quickly but carefully unzipped it to check on the elephants. They were all there and alive. They lifted their trunks and trumpeted at me happily. "Good to see you guys again, too," I said and donned the pack.

As Carl and I got into the elevator, I glanced up the corridor one last time. Freyja wasn't there, and neither was Arlene. As the doors closed, I caught a flash of a barefoot girl skittering across the hall carrying the rifle. *Good luck, Cassy*, I thought. For some reason, that made me grin. We were all just trying to survive.

PART FIVE

When I lay in bed now before sleep or during the sleepless intervals that seem to define these nights, I think about those we helped save, but even more about those we couldn't. The creatures who stood and watched as we rushed toward the crematorium exit. With all the doors unlocked, any of them could have joined us. I realize now it wasn't freedom from that room that they sought; it was freedom from this world. I have witnessed so many things that I never imagined I'd see. Now, I'm visited by the ghosts of these impossible moments that I'll never forget. Strangely, though, these visions also ignite hope. They force me to think of new ways forward, ways to piece together all of this madness and carve out something better.

Joe's Journal

PART FIVE

CHAPTER TWENTY-SIX

The helicopter raced low and steady over the Pacific. Helen, Max, and I lived on San Nicolas Island for the first six weeks. After the group became comfortable with their new habitat, we got an apartment in Port Hueneme, a few minutes from Naval Base Ventura County. Since we'd been forced to live in a one-room, two-bed barrack on the island, the move to living together on the mainland wasn't a huge decision. Helen and I got along well, and as we learned more about one another, our friendship grew. The remnants of Eve 19 that she carried were more curiosities than obstacles for both of us. Like the time I arrived home and found that she'd eaten a family-sized bucket of KFC but left all the meat, only consuming the extra crispy skin. That skin is tasty, so I get it. The fact that she gave into her cravings was a little worrisome, I suppose, but she assured me that if I didn't misbehave, she wouldn't flay me in my sleep. There was another time when she was slicing a bagel and the knife slipped, cutting a deep gash into the tip of her index finger, nearly to the bone. I couldn't convince her to go with me to urgent care, so we just dressed the cut. The next morning, the wound was almost completely healed, with only the slightest redness around the wound site.

I got a job at the Naval base as a supply chain specialist, which was a fancy term for stock boy, but I didn't mind. It allowed me free transport to the island a couple of times a week—mostly by boat, although sometimes I got to hitch a ride on a helicopter. I kept an inventory of the food and supplies needed for the group of over one hundred creatures that now roamed the various habitats on the south side of the island. I say "roamed," but most human hybrids had housing—converted shipping containers and FEMA trailers. Animals like Eddie the giant iguana, Tembo, and Smokey had plenty of space to stake as their territory while still being able to socialize with others when the mood struck them.

Otzi may have gotten the best spot on the island. They placed a FEMA trailer on a patch of land overlooking the ocean. It was only a short walk to the shoreline, and there, Otzi could fish to his heart's content. He insisted on using his traditional spear-fishing method at first, but once he finally tried a modern fishing pole, he never looked back.

We made sure he got all the latest gear and even built him a small grilling area on his patio so he could cook up his fresh catches. Boris and Smokey had a habitat that bordered Otzi's property, and the three of them hung out often. A soldier who does nighttime chopper patrols told me he has seen the three of them hanging out by Otzi's firepit late in the evening on several occasions. He described Otzi and Boris signing back and forth as Smokey lay content by the fire he'd helped to start.

Transitions to this new way of life weren't smooth across the board, however. Jaguarman's aggression remained high, and he wasn't satisfied with living "in captivity," as he called it, even with nearly half the island to roam. When pressed as to what he would like to do, he got frustrated. He seemed to realize that there wasn't a place in our current world for a half-jaguar, half-man creature. The same goes for Peter, to a lesser extent. Although he considered having his tail amputated, he just couldn't get himself to commit to that. He was living with it, for now, and making the best of the situation. He and Jaguarman got along, and I think their friendship was helping them cope.

Eddie had stopped growing, thank goodness. He's about thirty feet long now and eats from the abundant kelp beds just offshore. Michael, well, yeah . . . Michael. What does one do with an overly sexed turtle-spider-man creature? The obvious answer is "make another one of him," but, hopefully, the days of genetic manipulation like that were behind us. The next best thing we could think of was to provide him with an endless supply of porn. Just feed the addiction. Starving it certainly didn't seem like any way to live; plus, he wasn't hurting anyone by indulging in the whims of his true nature. He promised to keep to his hut while satisfying his urges. Needless to say, we didn't see much of Michael, but at least we knew he was happy.

The surfing gorillas were about the most well-adjusted members of the entire group. Kai, Bodie, Dax, Zach, Blaze, Maverick, and Grinder found the north-facing rocky coast to be a good spot for catching waves, especially during the fall and winter. The high surf generated by the storms that march down the coast wasn't quite Nazare big, but it was still challenging, even for those pros. They had their own little town, of sorts, built of stacked shipping containers and even a tiki hut that they built out of surplus lumber and materials from the Navy yard. Grinder still dreams of his skate park, and I've vowed to help him get it going somehow. He and I already have a location picked out in Oxnard for it, and my dad and I talked about what it might take to get investors. I don't know how it would all work out—a skate park run by a gorilla-human hybrid—but I know a goldmine when I hear it. Can you imagine how many people would line up to skate with a gorilla? Anyway, someday, maybe. In the meantime, we're having fun planning.

As far as the Basking brothers and their enterprises are concerned, Freyja didn't kill Bernard, but he was arrested and questioned while remaining locked up. That's all we were told, and I'm fine with it. The amount of data on Helen's phone, the videos and photos I took, and all the physical files at the Perfect Skin offices would take months or years to go through. It's our hope that science and medicine will eventually benefit from all the files and from Bernard himself, should the authorities get him to cooperate.

No one has located Albert yet. They found the medical room where Bernard operated on him, but no body or slurry of fluids matching Albert's description have been found. I'd like to think he dissolved into a puddle of plasma, but witnessing Bernard's capabilities in creating and reanimating life, I just don't know.

That leaves all the ladies formerly known as Eve. All had certain superhuman abilities, and the national security issues surrounding their creation and what they knew of the Baskings' operation were not trivial. But after about two months of talks, it was determined that they could live their own lives—provided they kept out of the public spotlight, stayed off social media, and learned the best way to hide their abilities and appearances. Some were like Helen, endowed with the ability to scale the "perfect" nature of their skin and radiance. Others were still very much a blend of their undersea and cosmic realms, their skin and striking appearance making it challenging for them to fit in. Makeup and choosing the right clothing helped. Some would have to lead rather sheltered existences until their appearances changed, if they ever did. Helen set up a monthly conference call with them and is working to get them the help they need through government-subsidized mental health and career assistance programs. Debbie's uncle James is pulling some strings on his end, as well.

Anyway, I can honestly say that I've found peace and I owe much of that to having my reality put through the blender. I don't know about you, but the decade of your twenties can be a tough one. Mine started out as one big party, and as parties go, it was pretty damn good. But I knew that I'd eventually have to move into adulthood. When I walked into the offices of Perfect Skin Dermatology for a mole check and ended up in a supernatural sideshow of biblical proportions, it forced me to change the way I thought about society, the world, even the universe. Most of all, it changed the way I thought about myself. It forced me to realize that I had far less control over my world than I thought. This opened my mind to accept chaos, uncertainty, and discomfort—three things I had actively avoided. It helped me realize that what matters most isn't nurturing the illusion of control but keeping my humanity intact when everything around me seems designed to strip it away. I found purpose in being part of something much larger, darker, and more complex than I had ever imagined.

CHAPTER TWENTY-SEVEN

Helen was in the kitchen feeding Max when I got home from work. She had just landed a nursing job at the Naval Ambulatory Care Center, and we were going to celebrate by going out to dinner.

"Can you see who that is on my phone?" she said loudly enough for me to hear from the living room.

I rushed into the kitchen and looked at her phone on the counter. "Sergeant Collins," I said. "Should I answer?"

She rose from scooping the dog food into the bowl and set the can next to the sink. "Sure, put him on speaker."

"Hi, Sergeant," Helen said.

"Hi, Helen. Hey, sorry to bug you. I know this is last minute, so if you can't make it, that's fine. A few of the guys on the base put together an impromptu barbeque thing on the island, and some regulars will be there.

Thought you and Joe might want to get a lift over with me and have a couple beers and some grub."

Helen looked at me, raised her eyebrows, and shrugged. I nodded enthusiastically.

"We're in!" Helen said.

"Great, I'll send a car over to pick you two up in an hour."

"Perfect, looking forward to it," Helen said and hung up.

"Think we should bring Max?" I asked, watching him finish the last of his food.

"Sure! Everyone loves Max!"

"And if they don't, he'll make them," I said.

She rolled her eyes at my joke, which was the perfect reaction.

Ninety minutes later, we were loading into the chopper, and thirty minutes after that, we were circling the far end of San Nicolas, coming in for a landing. The sun was just dipping into the water and there were just enough clouds to create a beautiful sunset.

The chopper arced and hugged the shoreline.

"Here's something I'm not sure I'll ever get used to seeing," the pilot said over our headsets. He dipped a little toward the sun and came in low. I squinted through the golden hues dancing over the water. Then I saw them: the six gorillas, five of them sitting on their boards, and Mohawk out front, paddling furiously to catch a good-sized wave. We watched as he stood, inched up the nose, and dipped into the trough. He ran his hand along the curl, and even though I couldn't quite see his face, I knew he was smiling.

EPILOGUE

Once he had made his way through the maze of storm drain channels and past the breakers at the mouth of the Santa Ana River, the crocodile swam gracefully, his tail slicing phosphorescent trails through the calm, predawn water. Although this river was colder than the salt water croc's native river in Papua New Guinea, it didn't bother Albert in the slightest. He was a tough creature, robust in structure, prehistoric in instinct, ruthless in pursuit. Albert tried to think like an ancient predator as he imagined the potential for his new host's power and ferocity. This new body would prove much more useful than his last. His days of navigating the banalities and limitations of terrestrial life were now behind him.

With Albert's brain inside the body of his prized pet Sobek, there was no end to the carnage he could inflict upon the world.

He was done with creating life. It was time to start removing the waste, starting with all his failed experiments. From the murky depths of ancient rivers to the shadowed alleys of modern cities to the broad Pacific, this planet wasn't prepared for the cleansing horror he would bring.

Man, it was good to be alive.

www.ingramcontent.com/pod-product-compliance
Lightning Source LLC
Chambersburg PA
CBHW010728100726
47899CB00009B/2972